Rapture

Joan Cooke (signature)

JOAN COOKE

Contents

Chapter 1 1

Chapter 2 3

Chapter 3 7

Chapter 4 10

Chapter 5 13

Chapter 6 15

Chapter 7 21

Chapter 8 32

Chapter 9 39

Chapter 10 44

Chapter11 52

Chapter 12 63

Chapter 13 74

Chapter 14 82

Chapter 15 87

Chapter 16 104

Chapter 17 110

Chapter18 118

Chapter 1

At the United Methodist Bible class early Wednesday afternoon, Reverend Paul commented that he saw on Twitter that buck-naked people were rising into the sky.

Millie, a God-fearing woman you would never forget, shouted in joyous ecstasy as she stumbled to her feet. "It's the Rapture, I tell you! Oh my God, It's the Rapture! Are we prepared? Quick take your clothes off."

Within seconds, the church group bursts from the building in a bewitched state, clothes flying through the air. Someone's panties sail into Ed's face. He grabs them and recognizes the garment. "Millie get your clothes on!"

"You heard Reverend Paul," she squealed. "It's the Rapture! It's happening all over the world. It's here! It's what we have been praying for! Ed get your eyes off the Bixtons' teen twins. Get your mind out of the gutter, this is the Rapture."

The church goers milled around with no directional sense, some falling over others, grabbing each other, doing the hip-hop shuffle.

"Look up the street, on the left," Millie yells, "See those people, looks like a naked family with their belongings folded on the ground beside them."

In unbelievable quickness the family ascends to the heavens. A hush swoops over the church group. To the right a few more people disappear!

"What about us?" Millie whispers. "We are not doing this right, everyone line up and put your clothes in a neat pile. Quiet, quiet."

The street empties, leaving a stunned group staring at their nakedness. Millie looks around; the twins are gone along with 9-year-old Roger. She is outraged. God has left her behind!

"You pervert!" she screamed, "You stinking heathen! This can't be right, I'm the most honest believer here, I'm righteous and do the Lord's work every day!"

"No, you bitch," someone bellowed, "you talk about everyone behind their backs! It's your fault we got left behind." The big man grabbed Millie by the neck and began squeezing the life out of her.

Ed reacted swiftly. A loud gunshot echoed and Millie's attacker fell in a pool of blood on the sidewalk!

As the shock wore off, there was a mad rush as everyone tried to cover their nakedness, ashamed to look at each other.

So it began.

Chapter 2

After a quick survey of the picture-perfect bedroom, she's satisfied that everything is in its place; the tight-fitting covers on the spotless smooth bed, the arrangement of gray and purple pillows at the top of the bed, and not an article of clothing in sight.

Having been raised in a military household, Josie was used to being controlled by time. She was usually up, showered, and dressed by exactly 7 a.m. The bedroom was clean and neat at 7:10 a.m. and breakfast was on the table by 7:20.

Josie finished breakfast and looked around; coffee, cereal and muffins littered the counters. Her first thoughts were to tidy up. No matter how hard she tried, she could not change the routine, so regimented was the pattern instilled in her mind as a child growing up with a dad who demanded perfection from his family 24/7. With a last swipe with the dish rag, Josie hung it up and glanced back at the kitchen. It met her approval.

She crossed the shiny beige tile floor, edged around the sparkling glass tabletop and stopped at the patio doors to look out at the view. She saw her three best friends from way back hanging around the pool in their colourful p.j.'s, drinking coffee and soaking up the early morning Florida sun.

Katie, a fun-loving brunette, had a purple stripe down the right side of her shoulder length hair. She was mostly agreeable but frowned easily and could be crusty with her opiniated outlook. She sat in a lawn chair with her flowery navy thrift store p.j.'s rolled up to her knees.

Bettie, lovable Bettie, questioned everything. She always came out strong, her way or no way. Betty talked about everyone but was loyal with a hidden agenda. She enjoyed eating and she rarely moved, hence or because of 290 pounds and 50E extra-heavy breasts. She quit everything she started, loved bright colours, and often sat in the shade as she did then, complaining about the heat.

Lynn was a quiet, mousy, 55-year-old slim woman who walked instead of rode at every opportunity. She dressed to perfection from hats to shoes. She always wore the right jewelry with the right outfit. opportunity, dresses to perfection from F right outfit. She said what she thought her listeners wanted to hear and viewed the world through rose-colored glasses. Lynn rarely talked about her family and was very loyal to her friends.

Josie wore pressed denim jeans and a white loose T-shirt. She carried a floral tote bag slung over her shoulder. Striding along in no-nonsense New Balance sneakers, she stepped onto the lanai.

"Where are you going" Bettie asked.

"I'm going to the shooting range," Josie called back, "can I drop anyone off at the mall or somewhere?"

"Thanks, but not after that long drive from Canada," Katie said. "I'm hanging around the pool today, this warm sunshine is soaking the cold out of these old northern bones."

"What do you mean?" Bettie asked. "You're going to the shooting range, is that a festival or what?"

"I'm going to practice my shooting; I've been slack the last couple weeks," Josie said.

"A gun!" Lynn chimed in, "you have a gun?"

"Yes," Josie replied.

"Josie, my god, you never, ever said or talked about a gun in all the years I've known you."

"Well, it's something I picked up when dad was in the armed forces," Josie said. "When I was a kid, 11 or 12, mom would send me with my brothers. It didn't matter if it was the baseball diamond or the shooting range, she thought I would be protected by my four older brothers. Plus, it kept me out of mischief. As you noticed I never learnt about fussy girl things, you know, like shopping, make-up and dresses."

"Yeah, we know; like when you watch TV, it's all hard ass, science fiction or detective stories," Katie said.

Lynn waved her hand. "Can I see it?"

"Yeah, me too!" Bettie said.

"Ok" Josie said, and slowly pulled her Glock out of her floral tote bag.

"Wow! It's a real gun." Katie exclaimed. "You had a gun in this house and never thought to mention it?"

"Can I touch it?" Bettie asked

"Bettie," Lynn squealed. "Are you insane?"

"It won't hurt you, the safety's on." Josie said.

"Yeah, yeah, tell that to all the kids that are accidentally shot in their homes," Katie muttered. "Yeah, it's safe up on a high shelf, locked in a steel box.".

"I'm not touching that thing!" Lynn said. "I've seen enough!"

Bettie and Katie stared in awe at the weapon. Lynn in disgust. Josie slid her gun back into her tote bag.

Katie broke the awkward moment. "Um, any of you see that weird stuff on TV last night, about people disappearing, like rising up into the air? I saw it on Fox News about 30 minutes or so, when I was making coffee."

"No, I haven't heard anything, but while I'm out, you guys check out different news channels," Josie said. "The BBC is best for true world news, keep track of what is going on, see if it's increasing or if it's fake news."

Chapter 3

A gust of hot air greeted Josie when she opened her car door. She slid into the seat, started the car, and promptly turned on the air - full blast.

"I love this Florida weather but it takes time to adjust from the cold north," she said. Josie fastened her seat belt and put on her glasses, then hit the road. She drove crosstown, up Midway Boulevard onto Tamiami Trail, and into the parking lot of Gun's Plus.

She swung the door open and ran into a fit, Marine-type guy who is around six-four, with a shaved head, a scowl, and a sneer in his brown eyes.

"Yeah, what do you want little lady? I think you are in the wrong place."

"Nope," Josie said, smiling as she stared him down. "I was told you had an excellent shooting range here."

"Yeah, what's it to ya?"

"I would like to practice." She said as she drew her Glock slowly from her tote.

"Lady, do you know what you are doing?"

"Yeah I do."

"I doubt it."

"Show me the way ... yes or no?"

He shook his head in disgust and asked for ID and insurance proof. Josie followed him through an entrance, down a staircase that smelled of gunfire and male sweat, into the most beautiful and organized shooting range she had ever seen.

After firing off a few rounds, Josie paused for a break. Sensing a movement behind her, Josie caught a whiff of fresh Dove with a trace of Old Spice and a faint odour of diesel. She lowered her Glock onto a shelf in front of her and slowly turned left. Josie brought her arms up as if stretching the muscles in her shoulders.

She used the movement to take in a man who looked to be in his 50s standing three feet behind her. He was clean-shaven with shoulder-length hair that framed a suntanned face and silver-blue eyes.

The man was dressed in a faded Hawaiian shirt that hung loosely over a pair of baggy knee length khakis that showed off a pair of muscular calves. He wore scuffed brown boat shoes; a brown leather man-bag hung loosely from his left shoulder.

He was watching Josie.

She took the initiative and shot out her hand. "Name's Josie."

"I'm Clint, he answered with a quiver of a smile, "I like your shooting."

Clint strode into the next cubicle, hung ear protectors on his head, drew his weapon and began to practice.

After another hour of practice firing, Josie parked her Glock in her tote bag. Out of the corner of her eye she saw Clint glance at her.

He moved to deposit his own weapon in his man-bag, then looked at Josie, hard.

He's flirting with me, Josie thought. I'm a fifty-five-year-old woman, a bit out of shape, short curly, dyed blond hair with an attitude more hostile than friendly. What do I do, this is unheard of?

Josie decided to take the bull by the horns. In a business-like manner she exchanged her protective glasses for her regular ones and straightened her clothes. She turned and headed out of the stall into Clint's space.

"You want to go for coffee?"

"Sure, where?" Clint answered.

"How about next door, there's a 50s diner there."

Chapter 4

As they stepped into the bright Florida sunshine, Josie snapped sunglasses onto her glasses. Clint glided across the parking lot with her, walking in straight measured steps as the breeze gently moved his hair. Oh, my God, she thought, am I interested or what?

"I haven't seen you here before," Clint said.

"No, it's new for me," he said. "I usually go to MT's in Englewood on Wednesdays."

"Yeah, MT's place, I know it well." He opened the door for her and they entered the coolness of the diner.

Marks for good manners, Josie thought.

"You want a booth or a table?"

"A booth is good."

Clint walked to the booth, waved at the waitress, and nodded at several guys.

"How does a slice of pie or a donut sound?"

"Lemon pie would be great!"

"Set it up, Stacy, two coffees and two slices of that melt-in-your-mouth lemon pie," Clint called out to Stacy as he slipped into a booth with his right side facing the aisle.

Josie slid in opposite him with her bag tucked on her right side.

"I saw you score 9.89," Clint commented, "where did you learn that calm precision from?"

"I was raised with four older brothers on military bases across the country," she replied. "Mom thought it would keep me out of mischief and my brothers would watch out for me if I went to the shooting range weekly with them. And you?"

Before Clint could answer, the diner door crashed open. A stoned unkempt 30ish man tore into the room, leading a trio of nasty thugs.

"Stacy, you cheating whore, get your sorry ass out here!" A shot was fired and the report echoed through the diner. On perfect cue, Josie and Clint reached into their bags and pulled out their weapons.

In between screaming, flying food and drinks, everyone dived for cover behind overturned tables. Josie aimed at the first guy and shouted, "STOP!"

He froze on the spot and looked at Josie with a bewildered expression as his buddies crashed into him. They fell to the floor. A shot rang out and a light fixture shattered.

Clint shot out of the booth and calmly took the weapons from the men entangled on the floor. "Gentleman, please sit yourselves along the wall," he said as he pointed his gun at them.

Josie stepped up next to Clint, her weapon pointed as a second warning.

* * *

After an hour of police questioning, Clint and Josie were allowed to leave the diner. Josie turned towards Clint. "You want to go out for dinner tonight, sort of unwind?"

"I am thrilled you asked. I know a quiet restaurant."

"Yeah that's what you said about the diner."

Clint reaches out, gently takes Josie's hand, giving it a soft squeeze. "Bye for now, see you at Phil's on Tamiami Trail around 7."

Chapter 5

Josie arrived home to find the girls still on the lanai, playing cards in their swimsuits and enjoying drinks and snacks.

"Hey girls, how ya'll doing?" Josie asked.

"We're cool," Bettie said. "You're later than we figured."

Josie told them what happened, mentioning more than once the handsome guy she met. "I have a meeting with Clint at 7 at Phil's."

"A date!" screamed Katie.

"No, no, not a date, I'm going for a shower, see you later." Josie answered.

"Josie has a date, huh, huh," sang Katie. "K-I-S-S-I-N-G, first comes love, then comes..."

"Oh for God's sake, shut up!" Josie snapped back. "It's a meeting to go over the day's events; he's a nice guy."

"A nice guy?" Lynn asked. "I see a sparkle in your eyes,"

"And a swing in those hips," Katie added.

After Josie's shower and a much-needed nap, she dressed quickly.

As she returned to the lanai Lynn shrieked, "Josie, you're not wearing that!"

Josie, dressed in blue denim shorts, a blue T-shirt and blue sneakers, asked, "Why not?"

"For God's sake, it's a date, A DATE," Lynn answered. "Get your white crocheted skirt and hey, wear my white sparkly V-neck and my white sandals."

Katie jumped in. "And earrings, Josie, here, have my drop turquoise ones and add my silver and turquoise bracelet, they're in my room."

The girls surrounded. "Did you shave your legs?"

"Yeah, when I showered." Josie answered.

"Thank God, you did something right." Lynn commented.

"Let me do your make-up." Katie insisted.

"I already put on lipstick." Josie commented.

"Well, you look undone." Katie said.

"Nonsense."

"What kind of panties are you wearing?" Bettie asked.

"What? My regular white cotton ones."

"No, no, no, let's look through your dresser," Bettie demanded.

"No way, they are all the same!"

"I have a pair of black cotton ones," Josie said.

"Well that's better than white cotton, so old and so original," Bettie said. "We will have to get you some lacy undies, put it on your shopping list."

After plenty of give and take, the girls placed Josie in front of the full-length mirror.

"Well, well, I really look pretty," Josie marveled. "Thanks guys, thanks a million. I feel a tingle on my heart."

Bettie piped in, "Probably in the nether regions too!"

Chapter 6

Josie drive her charcoal grey Venza SUV into the full parking lot at Phil's on Tamiami Trail, known as Highway No. 41 in Punta Gorda. Seeing a parking space ahead she inched towards it when a red Mustang barrels past to take the space. But suddenly it stopped and backed out.

There must be a motorcycle or debris blocking the spot, Josie thought. As she moved closer to the space, she saw what was blocking the spot. Clint standing in the space. He wore black slacks, a pale lemon-coloured shirt with sleeves rolled up, several buttons undone and a thin gold chain around his neck. He saw Josie and motioned her into the space.

Once she was parked, he leaned in and opened her door.

"Josie girl, be more ladylike," she thought. Josie accepted his extended hand as another thought raced through her head: I wonder if he's just as nervous as I am?

They walked into the restaurant, chit-chatting about the day. The hostess winked at Josie and escorted the couple to an oversized round booth. Josie slid in first; Clint was right behind her. She edged over a bit; he edged even closer.

He's putting on the moves, she thought, I like!

You're looking beautiful tonight," Clint said.

"You clean up pretty nice yourself."

He grinned. "By your accent I assume you're Canadian, are you on holidays?"

"Yes, from Ontario, a small town called Sauble Beach on Lake Huron about five and a half hours north of Detroit. I'm down here on a girls' trip with three friends whom I have known for 30 years plus."

"I'm a full-time Southerner," Clint said. "I hear it can be cold and nasty up north. I'm a P.I., semi-retired. I take small jobs here and there."

The waitress took their drink orders, then Clint continued.

"Port Charlotte has lots of gated communities and rentals for snowbirds. It's a quiet town without the hustle and bustle of noisy family orientated resorts with amusement parks. I try to make a point of spending time here between jobs. I enjoy my leisure time, after sailing on the Gulf, sometimes fishing for the big catches.

"I've had a house off Midway for seven years now," Josie said. "Coming down with the girls gives me a chance to check it out before I come down for the winter. I am retired and so are the girls."

"Your husband, does he mind?"

"Widowed, five years now."

"I'm sorry to hear that," Clint said. He paused for a moment. "You know, I never did find the number one."

Josie made some small talk, then mentioned the news story about the naked people floating up to the skies. "Do you think it's true?"

"I heard about it, I might check it out," Clint said.

While consuming an appetizing dinner of coconut shrimp, they discussed the shooting incident at the diner.

"I'm impressed with your skills, when did you begin handling guns?"

"Raised in a family of four brothers with a stay-at-home mom and a dad in the military, it was the natural flow of life. I did what the boys did. Like if dad was taking them on a hike, mom sent me along with them, she was kind of antisocial. That was just the way it was, I knew no different...hunting shooting and fishing. No girly things for me, I guess I would make a good spy."

But enough about me, Josie thought. "So, are you originally from this area?" she asked.

"I'm one of the few Florida natives," Clint answered readily. "Raised here in Florida. I like the wild parts. The seashore was my home. Just mom and me, I don't remember my dad. Mom was happy to let me wonder. She died when I was nineteen. I inherited enough money to travel. Then I went to work for the St. Petersburg police department. I retired after twenty-five years, bought a boat, and got my private investigator's license."

They talked more about Clint's boat at the marina and his job as a P.I. Josie opened up about her retirement, the passing of her husband of thirty years and her girlfriends. It feels like we are connected, she thought later, as she agreed to join Clint for a drive over to see his boat.

* * *

Josie gulped as she stared at Clint's boat—it was a yacht. Not a boat, a floating luxury hotel.

Clint took Josie's arm and guided her aboard. They paused at the first step on the deck, embraced and exchanged a passionate kiss, their arms entangled around each other. Slowly Josie freed herself, removed her sandals and glided across the smooth polished teak deck. She paused to take in the clear sky with the sun setting on her left, creating ribbons of rose and orange that moved across the water, sparkling like diamonds where the waves softly breached the surface,

She grasped the smooth white railing with a gentle hold as a huge sailboat glided into the marina, gently rocking Clint's boat. The sailboat furled its sails, the masts left glowing gold in the sunset

A fishing trawler, painted in glossy blue, red and white, chugged slowly behind the sailboat, a handful of seagulls circling it. The fishermen waved and Josie waved back happily.

Clint stepped up behind Josie and rested his warm hands on her buttocks. She turned and lifted her face towards him, as he moved into her arms, giving Josie a soul-loving kiss. She trembled as she returned his kiss with hot desire, caught in a well of fantasy.

She caught her breath, moaning in soft purrs as she leaned into Clint. I would stumble without his strong arms supporting me, she thought, as Clint guided her through the living area to a massive bed. Soon she was lying on top of him, her emotions spinning out of control. That last kiss lit a fire in the core of her soul. Driven by lust, she yielded to the inevitable.

Later she lay comfortably in his arms, getting her breath under control as he, too, gasped for air. She looked into his eyes and he smiled. Josie smiled in return, at peace. The gentle rocking of the boat lulled them to sleep.

She woke alone on the bed, the smell of coffee around her and a bright blue blanket covering her., Her head had a bit of a sonic buzz, as if she had been drinking heavy. She washed and dressed, then looked in the mirror and saw a happy satisfied woman. Josie headed into the deck and smiled as she accepted a mug of hot coffee from Clint,

"Thanks, sailor."

They chowed down a light breakfast of scrambled eggs with cheese and a toasted English muffin glazed with butter and strawberry jam. Sitting over a second cup of coffee, Josie mentioned the buzz in her head. Clint said "I've had that feeling every now and then. My job down here is to investigate the phenomena of the disappearing people. I've read that the sensation is part of the disappearing process."

They chatted for a while, but the missing people were really the farthest from their minds. Instead they stared unto each other's eyes, randomly touched, and otherwise enjoyed the company. She told him her plans for the immediate future.

"I'm going to hang around with the girls for three to four weeks, then we'll head north up 1-75." Josie handed him a small post card with her address and phone number here in Port Charlotte. On the card she placed a tiny pin with a red maple leaf embossed on it. Clint gave her his cell number. Later he drove her back to the restaurant to pick up her car. They talked non-stop as if they could not say or listen enough. At Josie's car they parted with hugs, kisses, and promises of future encounters.

She drove slowly, stunned as she noticed groups of naked people standing on corners, no panic, just quietly waiting. Waiting for what though? The ascendance into heaven or what? Josie was tempted to call Clint, but she felt sort of foolish about running after him so soon. Although the naked people merited investigation, she blushed as she realized she really wanted the detective to continue his intimate investigation of her.

Chapter 7

At home, Bettie and Katie were frantic as they greeted Josie.

"Has the world gone crazy?"

"Where have you been?" Katie yelled. "Oh, I know by that glow on your face and the sparkling eyes, I know...but so much is going on. All the news channels are carrying stories of the disappearances. No one knows why the religious groups are claiming it's the rapture. Talk shows are claiming terrorists, mumbling of a government test gone wrong."

"Where's Lynn?" she asked.

"We have her tied up in the bed room," answered Katie.

"What?"

Katie speaks very slowly. "Josie, honestly I don't know what's going on with Lynn. We were on the lanai sitting quiet when she jumped up and started tearing her clothes off. I mean, stripped naked, Josie, completely naked."

Bettie chimed in. "Then she ran out towards the street. We grabbed her and fought for control, brought her into the house but she was wild, scratching, kicking and swearing at us four times before we found some garden twine in the garage and tied her up."

"We added loops of orange extension cord to stop her," Katie said. "She kept repeating 'I must wait for them, out there.' She was screaming, it was horrible, we had to gag her."

Katie was upset not only because of Lynn, she told Josie, but also because she could not reach her family up north by phone or e-mail.

"And there seems to be an electromagnetic pulse beating in my head," Josie said.

"Yeah, an electronic transmission in my head too, saying something I don't understand," Bettie replied. "You think that's what's in Lynn's head? Josie you left us here alone in a strange town, no way to go for help or to leave. I hate you. You think you can go have fun and leave us alone? I'm scared Josie, really scared."

Josie stepped back a few paces and tried Clint's number on his cell - just static.

"Girls be quiet, let me think, let me hammer this out," she said to her friends. Josie felt total responsibility for them. It was at her insistence that they came to Florida. She sat and pondered but found it hard to even concentrate. My head is full of static, she thought, what in the world is happening? She stood, sat down, then rose again. She tried to control her thoughts. She walked into the bedroom to check on Lynn. She lay on the bed thrashing madly, pulling at the cords binding her as she mumbled unintelligible sounds.

Josie returned to the kitchen, grabbing her head and shaking as she sit down. Then Josie started counting, from 25 then down to 1 and calling the alphabet out loud. She began repeating an old nursery rhyme as Katie and Bettie stared in confusion. "As long as I'm doing this crazy number, letter nonsense, the static goes down by ninety or more percent."

She got Katie and Bettie to the table. "Sit down. Talk to yourselves, sing up and down musical scales, count to one hundred, don't worry if you miss a number, just think out loud!"

"This is good," Katie said moments later, "I don't feel like I'm going crazy with that awful static, thanks Josie."

"This is stupid, really nuts, Josie," Bettie said. "Oh, oh, I'll work at it."

They went back into Lynn's bedroom where she was still twisting and screaming at herself. They continued reciting nonsense.

"Katie, hold Lynn's hands."

Josie tried to get her to start counting numbers. "1,2,3,4,5...16,17,18,20. Come on Lynn, look up, lets chant the alphabet together. A, B, C, D, E.

After a second or two they saw a glimmer of intelligence in Lynn's eyes. "Girls. Let's count together, 1,2,3,4, Lynn, count with us, 5,6,7."

Lynn opens her dry mouth and joins in, "8,9,10."

"Keep it up you girls, we'll win this battle yet." Bettie gave Lynn a sip of water as they continued the counting. When they hit one hundred she nudged Katie. "Stay with Lynn, keep counting, we'll switch off each other every five minutes."

Twenty-five minutes later Lynn was back to normal. Bettie helped her dress, continuing the reciting now and then. Josie called the girls to the kitchen to make lunch. They all sang old songs, counted, and talked even as they ate because it lessened the horrible mind pull.

Is God talking to them? Josie thought. Is it the rapture? Is it a predisposition? Is it hysteria? Are we less susceptible than Lynn? Will we ascend too? Why? Let me think, if the majority are subdued, what happens to the rest? Civilization is threatened. How will society function? Questions, questions and no answers.

"Girls, I want you to listen to me with an open mind," Josie finally said. "We have seen people ascend into the sky. Girls, this is it, I think we are all, I mean the whole world, at the mercy of something that wants us. Whether it's God or what, I don't know, all I know is we must fight it. We know the steady counting stops the static, the static that caused Lynn to want to join the departed. If we work hard and watch each other we'll control our lives. We don't have to accept the invitation to the dance."

"Josie, how do you know that we are not invited?" Bettie whispered.

"Because, we are not like Lynn, like all those standing naked on the street waiting. Let's take a quick walk up the street, remember to chant, hold hands and help each other out. Take extra notice of Lynn."

They hesitated at the door, uncertainty showing on their faces. We are scared! Josie thought.

"Girls, no hemming or hawing," she said. "All for one! Let's do it. "

Out they stumbled, down the sidewalk then down the driveway. The street was quiet beneath cloudy skies. No, not clouds, murky blurred shadows rising straight into the air.

"Look to the right. What do you see?" Without a sound a cluster of people ascended to the heavens. They backed up, hands held tight, and ran for the house.

"Quick, quick, lock it," Bettie screamed as they piled back into the house. They locked the door, got the booze out of the cupboard and poured doubles all around. Everyone was shaken!

"I know it's terrifying, monstrous, but we must do this," Josie said. They lifted their drinks, clicked glasses, and downed their poison in one gulp. They poured another round and sat at the table.

"We are going to make a list of supplies and hunker down till the sonic sounds are gone, our lives depend on this," Josie said. "Girls, if we hide out for three or four weeks with enough food and water, it could be possible that the disappearances are over. How about everyone take a break, have a drink, think about it. I'll begin making a shopping list." Josie and the girls soon compiled a list of food, water and drinks needed for four weeks, plus gas, bullets and hygiene products.

After twenty minutes of shocked conversation the girls drifted back to the table. Josie photocopied the lists with blank spaces for anyone to add. She also hauled everything out of the liquor cupboard and set up glasses and ice.

"I think this is a good time for a healthy shot of your favourite drink. Time is important."

Bettie slammed herself into a chair and grabbed a Bud Light. "This better be good."

Lynn slid into the chair across from Josie and nabbed a beer. Katie joined them after mixing a rum and coke. All stared open-mouthed at the news reports on the television and radio.

"I'll take a double ginger ale with ice," Josie said. "We want to do this fast then off to shopping. As you can see on the news and right here on our street, it appears that something is driving people crazy then snatching them up into the sky. It could be a foreign government or our government or a big business or alien, I don't know. I just know I plan to survive."

"I see that the list reads; canned meat, canned veggies, canned fruit, and puddings, no fresh stuff," Bettie said.

Josie, "We'll get eight or nine days' fresh produce, some fresh meat maybe more. Think ahead of the fridge and freezer dying."

"What do you mean, dying?" Bettie asked.

"I predict power could fail."

"Are you out of your mind? Bettie asked. "How can you think of such a horrible thing?"

"It is possible that the world is going to change and not for the better," Josie replied.

"I see water on the list," Katie said. "You want lots of big gallon-size containers and lots of cases and small bottles, yes I understand that, drinking."

"Also, washing, brushing teeth, etc. if the electric grid fails."

"It seems the whole thing hinges on the electricity," Katie said. "What about the toilets?"

"We can draw water from the pool to flush the toilets," Josie said.

"What's this tons of newspaper and a hundred black plastic garbage bags and loads of duct tape?" Bettie asked.

"We need to cover the windows in preparation of hungry, gun-carrying wandering people," Josie said. "Girls this is a do or die situation, do you all understand? We stand together, if one of us falls, we could all die. The fact is I've planned a four-week schedule of food and water, mostly canned. When the electricity fails, and it will with no people operating the system, it will probably run for a period of time in its own automatic setups, but I have no idea how long. Each of you will get what's on your list, plus a few of your favourites."

"What about money?"

"I can pay on my debit card," Josie said. "Read the list over, think about it, we'll meet back at the table in 10 minutes."

The girls are shocked, as well they should be, living a carefree life of plenty then bang, it was over. Josie brought her memories and upbringing to the centre of her mind as she talked to the girls about survival. "We live or die, we are on our own."

"You're mean," Bettie said, "downright selfish."

"I want to live."

"What about snacks like potato chips, popcorn and candy?" Lynn asked. "I see you have five cases of soda pop on my list."

Katie and Lynn chimed in, "And on my list."

"Yes, pick out a dozen or more chips, the kind you like, candy too."

"What about personal stuff, hygiene things like pads and medication?" Bettie asked.

"Yes, each of you pick up what you need for four or five weeks, include any booze you want," Josie said. "When the time is up and we head north the stores will be empty. My list includes meats, fresh veggies and fruit. We'll go to Publix and load up. If we don't have enough, we can go to Walmart."

They drove through semi-empty streets with lots of vehicles stopped against the curbs with doors hanging open. A low breeze stirred up colourful items of discarded clothing into piles against palm trees and car tires. They pulled into Publix, parking close to the doors, and jumped out of the SUV. They rushed through, grabbed carts and began on the list. Soon everyone is back at the checkout except Bettie.

Josie went looking and found her standing by the shelf of canned meats and fish.

"Bettie, what are you doing?"

"I'm reading the labels."

"What part of 'This is an emergency' did you not understand?" Josie snaps. She swept her arms along a stack of tuna, knocking the whole row into her cart.

"What, what, don't you care about what you are eating?" Bettie squealed.

Josie piled cans of Spam and other processed meats into her cart.

"That's a lot more than what was on my list," Bettie said.

"Forget the numbers on your list, just fill the cart and get another one for water, then we can move on," Josie said. She ran back to the checkout in time to ring Katie out. Lynn who was almost ready at another checkout yelled out, "I got five ice creams." She was pleased with herself and right in the game.

Josie raced back to the canned veggie aisle and quickly loaded two carts, then arrived back at the checkout as Bettie wheeled up her carts.

They paid, then pushed their carts to the SUV, loading her as fast as they could. There was barely room for the girls.

They headed home in high spirits until they saw a huge group of people vanishing upwards. The streets seemed more deserted. They unloaded, a chore in itself. Everyone was tired.

"Listen up," Josie said. "Take a nap, relax, I'm heading out."

"Don't leave us," Lynn cried.

"You're going to be OK," Josie said. "Lock the doors, open only for me. I'll be back as quick as I can."

She went to the hardware store for pails, shovels, hunting knives, and then to the gun store for a huge supply of ammunition and a few guns. After another unsettling drive home, she used her key to enter. It was quiet and the girls were sleeping. Good, I have a big job ahead, she thought, convincing the girls to tape over the windows, blocking out everything outside.

Josie started the barbeque. She prepared steaks, chopped onions and mushrooms, then cleaned and wrapped potatoes in tinfoil. She mixed up a huge fresh veggie salad and grabbed ranch and Thousand Island dressing from the cupboard. She popped the potatoes on the hot grill, added mushrooms and onions with olive oil to the cast iron frying pan, and set them on the grill.

Waiting for the vegetables to cook, Josie turned on the computer searching for news about the event. The girls stepped into the kitchen one by one. Josie suggested they make a teeny drink and sit out on the lanai while she grilled the steaks. Lynn moved into the kitchen, opening and closing cupboard doors as she set the table.

"Let's eat, then sort out this warehouse of goods, see if we need to go for more supplies," Josie said.

After two hours or so of sorting, marking, and storing food in bedrooms and hallways, they decided to drive to Walmart to buy a few items, mostly medications plus a couple dozen magazines and a load of pocket books. They picked out backpacks for each of them.

Following a restless night, they spent the whole day covering the windows with newspaper and black plastic garbage bags.

"It's like a prison in here," Bettie said.

"We need to hide from desperate people," Josie said. She made a three-inch hole at the top of the living room window facing the street, moved the couch, and then placed a stepladder there to easily observe. She did the same in the dining room patio door.

The women set up a watch, day and night, two at a time watching and listening. They marked in notebooks the sounds of gunshots. Josie explained the gunshot count, with the idea that they'll lessen and when they stop, the women would head out for home, north up 1-75.

They had their first scary event at 2 a.m. on the third night. Bettie came running into Josie's room, whispering and out of breath. "Josie, are you awake? Josie, there's a mob out there shooting like mad, I'm scared."

Josie slipped out of bed. Yes, loud bangs, rolling one after the other. She listened for several minutes, then advanced swiftly into the living room. "It's thunder, I'm pretty sure."

"Pretty sure?" Bettie asked. "Yes or no, it is or it isn't gunfire."

Josie waved at the girls to be quiet, although she didn't really have to, they were shocked. The truth was sinking in. Josie walked to the front window, climbed the ladder and peeked outside. She saw flashes of lightning. She climbed down and walked to the front door.

"No, Josie, no!" Katie said.

"Quiet everyone," Josie said. She slowly swung the door open. Lightning flashed and thunder banged out with steady rhythm.

Chapter 8

On the fifth day they stopped using the BBQ. The odour of the cooking meat could attract unwelcome guests. Josie warned the girls about smoking outside as it may bring bad guys. It was hard on Bettie, a chain smoker and Lynn, who smokes three or four smokes a day. Josie was constantly on the smokers' case causing tempers to run high.

"Katie, you used my toothpaste," Bettie screamed

"No, I didn't and you left the bathroom a mess," Katie fired back.

Josie moved to separate Bettie and Katie, sending them to their rooms.

"Who died and made you boss?" howled Bettie.

"Quiet," Lynn spoke up. "If you don't stop the evil meanies will come."

That slowed down the conflict. About an hour later, Josie called everyone together. "I'm going outside, you can all come with me." Bettie and Lynn shook their heads and waved at Josie; they decided to go sit on the lanai. Katie stood at the open front door. Josie sneaked across the lawns of five homes to the main cross street, then slipped around the corner and up against the first house and around the house. Then she crept around a car. The street was quiet with a few sounds humming away.

'Nothing to report," she said after completing her reconnaissance. The power was still on but there were no newscasts. Mostly the women watched satellite TV, old movies and sitcoms. They kept the sound down low and whispered to each other.

They were scared and looked to Josie for guidance. They stopped using their cell phones and the land line trying to connect with family up north. No good results, just static! They worried about the disappearances, what is its purpose, would they be next? Would they be taken in their sleep? Would they die in Florida, unable to reach family and friends?

They were all on edge. Soon the tension took its toll on the friends. Petty arguments opened up and ended just as quickly. The large house, fortunately, offered places where they could disappear to cry or vent. They continued to double-check the sight holes, do quick neighbour scans, and slip outside for a quick peek before scurrying back inside.

And they always traveled in twos—two on the lanai while another two manned the sight lines. They grew sad, distressed, and felt the isolation of no phone lines, no television or computer links. Josie thought about Bettie and Lynn, smokers, trying to do without. But sometimes she did catch a whiff of smoke on Bettie's clothes.

***

Two weeks later the electric grid went down completely. The girls hadn't seen anyone, but they had heard lots of noise—screams, gunshots, and dogs yelping and howling in the distance. The static had disappeared, but in its place was a strange stillness. They see nobody, no groups of people, no solitary person, nada. Strange how quiet it was, except for a low hum. They soon found the source- -two houses along the street with air conditioners running off a generator. Josie sneaked up to the huge stucco building, checked out the pool area, and peeked in the uncovered windows. She saw no sign of life.

Josie located the generator on the outside of the garage and shut off the whole system. Quiet, total quiet. It made her blood run cold. As she crept toward home, she saw movement. Her breath caught, then she relaxed. It was just a bright yellow and blue shirt wrapped around a pole. The street was littered with colourful clothing, lying like damp dishrags, abandoned and discarded on the streets. There was no breeze. She quickly stepped back a dozen steps or more. Suddenly she heard dogs in the background.

Back home, it was Josie's turn on the lanai with Katie. For some reason, the tension of the dull, close house dribbled away. She relaxed in the brown lawn chair, semi-drifting, when she heard voices. She jumped to her feet and grabbed Katie,

"Shhh," she whispered frantically.

"I tell you, I smell fresh cig smoke," they heard a man growl in a deep, gruff voice. "Someone is alive hereabouts, within sniffing distance. Take a deep breath, you smell that?"

"Only on my clothes," answered a second man.

Katie and Josie sneaked into the house, locking the door behind them. Katie signaled Bettie and Lynn. Josie ordered Lynn up the ladder at the living room window. Katie went to her station at the peephole near the floor at the back of the house. Josie grabbed her pistol, slipped it into her waistband, and moved toward the back of the house.

"Someone is out there."

"Good, I'm so glad, maybe we are being rescued," Bettie whined. "Delivered from this living hell!"

"Bang, bang," two hard blows rocked the door, then there was silence. Suddenly Lynn screamed as she almost fell from her perch.

"See, I told you," shouted the gruff-voiced man. "Open this door or I'll blow it apart."

Katie ran into the kitchen and crouched on the flood. Lynn climbed down from the ladder and stood at the end of the sofa close to the door. Josie drew her gun and stood with the sofa between her and the door. Bettie walked to the door, unlocked it, and slowly opened it.

A huge, hairy man ripped the door from her hands, yanking it with such force it was torn from the jamb.

"Well, well lookie we found ourselves a sexy one," said the big man.

"Yeah and a tiny hottie," said his pal, looking towards Lynn.

Bettie walked up. "Glad to see somebody from the government."

"Yeah baby, I got your government," the hairy one said as he cupped his genitals in a crude gesture.

Missing the gesture, Bettie reached out to hug her rescuer. He grabbed her top and tore it off her body, then leered. Bettie screamed, rocked to her senses by the violence and what it implied. Lynn, meanwhile has already been stripped of her shorts by the second man, who gleefully pulled down his own drawers.

Soon they are all on a tangle on the floor. Bettie struggled, yelling "You fucker, you fucker." A fist emerged from the tangle, socked Bettie in the face, then pounded her several times. She fainted.

Josie rose from behind the sofa. She slowly removed the safety on her gun. She had no choice. In a fleeting moment she thought of all the practice, all the shooting at paper targets and tin cut-outs. But this was a human., No, he was not, he was a monster intent on destroying her and her friends, she reasoned, all in seconds. She brought her gun down an inch, aimed, then fired. The bullet exploded into the left side of hairy guy's head. A geyser of blood, brains and bone burst out of what was left of the thug's head. The second mad rose and turned to run, but tripped over his underpants, which were still down around his ankles. Josie shot him in the back of the head, pitching him half in, half out of the front entranceway.

Katie scurried out of the kitchen, white-faced and trembling.

"What's done is done," Josie said.

Lynn crawled to her feet. "Oh Josie, you were great!"

Katie and Josie began caring for Bettie. They soon stripped off her torn, bloodstained clothing and began bathing her.

"She is going to have a rainbow of colours on her face," Katie remarked.

Bettie came to as they washed her, spouting foul words and sputtering shrilly.

***

Hours later, Josie had dragged the bodies outside and dumped them into the hedges. She came back into the living room, where the girls had managed to place the door back into the jamb and close it. She sat down at the quick meal on the table—an open can of peas, some crackers, tuna, a handful of cheese and some old tarts. Four bottles of water and a flask of Gatorade served as libations. But the odour of the newly dead, strong urine and stinky feces, led them to leave the good food untouched.

Turning from the table, Lynn vomited onto the floor as she gagged and gasped out apologies. "I'm sorry, so sorry."

"Gals," Josie said, "this is not a game, time to back up and head out."

"Out, out there?" Bettie squealed. "We'll all be killed."

"Lynn, look at me," Josie said. "Bettie, grab some towels, cover that mess. Lynn look at me."

Josie took Lynn's ice-cold hands in hers and give her a gentle pull. "Lynn, listen to me, we're leaving soon. Hey, girl. I can't promise better in the future, but I can promise love and protection today and maybe forever."

She nodded dully. Josie looked around the room and made eye contact in turn with each of the women. "We gotta go, girls," she said. One by one, they all nodded in agreement.

Chapter 9

In the dark of night, Josie stepped out the door connecting the garage to the house and pushed the button to lift the garage door. It screeched like a banshee as it rose to open, breaking the still of the early morning. While the girls hauled food into the garage, she backed the SUV through the open door into the garage. They packed two weeks' worth of food into the back of the Venza, then stuffed what was left on the floor and anywhere else they could find.

Josie pointed to her backpack, one of four the women had packed for themselves. "The backpack goes with us, no matter how long we are away from the car," she said. "It is our support system."

Bettie attempted to lift her pack. "Why, why, is it so heavy and bulky. I can't carry this!"

"Let me check your pack," Josie said. "Bettie, you have too much food. Listen, for the first few days we will share, if you open a can of meat, we all have some, then Lynn opens a veggie, Katie opens a fruit, so the cans are not left open and wasted." She rummaged through Bettie's overstuffed pack. "Bettie, Bettie, you have tons of Poise pads, and what are these? Knick-knacks, a book?"

"I need all of it," Bettie said. "The knick-knacks aren't they cute?"

"Why?"

"Some for my grandkids, you know, good pieces," Bettie chirped.

"Let's divide the Poise between us," Josie said with a sigh. "Hope for the products in the stores. It may come to the fact that we need to tear up rags for pads. Remember, if you become separated, or lose the car, we need the back packs, it's your life line! We can't count on help. At the end of the day, it is up to each of us to plan, prepare and be ready. The ability to survive rests solely on you, take time to study and understand the danger, maintain awareness at all times. Don't count on the government coming to our aid, disasters bring out the worst in people."

They checked one another's packs for the essentials: flashlights, water, a change of underwear, and a first-aid kit. Josie made sure to pack her 9 mm Glock 17 pistol plus extra ammo. She carried her Ruger 10/22 rifle to the SUV. On the floor of the car she placed several boxes of ammo. Then, as a final touch, she painted a large red maple leaf on the wall in the living room.

* * *

Finally, they were ready. They gathered their courage and climbed into the SUV in silence, placing their backpacks near them. At 3 a.m. they pulled out of the garage, heading up Lackworth.

We'll will travel as far as we can," Josie said. "Katie, you watch ahead, anything moving, yell out, keep your glasses on. Lynn, are you OK? I want you to watch our tail end, make an opening through the stuff in the back so you can see. Bettie,

40

please watch the right side, check outwards and keep an eye on the mirrors. I'll drive and watch the left."

Bumper-to-bumper traffic usually filled all lanes of Highway 41. But it was eerily quiet. The only sound was the car's engine. They traveled through the empty town, bright sunlight shining, with the acrid smell of smoke in the stale air.

"There up ahead," Katie called out, "two people pushing a loaded grocery cart!"

Josie slowed down a bit and passed them, they don't even look up. The traffic lights are working, maybe operating on solar panels. Abandoned cars parked along the road, no people, a pack of dogs at a distant street crossing. Suddenly a gunshot ripped the quiet. The women all jumped. Josie drove faster.

They started up the ramp to 1-75 when a loud buzzing began in everyone's head.

Lynn grabbed at the car doors.

"Lynn, Lynn." Katie pulled Lynn back from leaping out of the SUV.

"Everyone remember, ABC's ... 1,2,3's, count in your minds, don't let this thing in."

Bettie whimpered. "I'm scared, I thought we would be done with this sonic buzzing thing."

"I don't know how long it will be," Josie said.

"I know you are driving into the danger," Bettie said.

"Bettie, listen, everyone listen up, we can't stay here," Josie said angrily. Why didn't they get it? "The world that we know has ended. Our only hope we have is to head north, north towards home!"

They drove on, past abandoned cars, piles of clothing—lots of clothing—wrapped around cars and posts. They were terrified; they were looking at a world empty of people. After three hours and sixty miles or so, Josie pulled off the interstate at exit 214. The sign said Ellenton.

They stopped at the convenience store. It had not been ransacked. They took care of that, grabbing chocolate bars, pop, water, and chips. After using the rest room, they climbed back into the car. Everyone had perked up. Farther down the road they came across three houses set near the road. They drove into the first laneway which was deserted.

"Bettie and Katie, remember the plan," Josie said. "You two scout out the back, Lynn and I will check the front. Remember your backpacks."

"Nag, nag, nag. She thinks we are children, who made her boss?" Bettie muttered. She tried the sliding door at the back. It was unlocked. She slid it open. Hot, musty air blew out.

As Katie and Bettie entered the house, Katie said, "Remember the practice, check all closed doors, check rooms."

"Lynn, what are you waiting for?" Josie whispered. Lynn opened the front door and stepped quietly into the house. As she creeped in, Josie followed closely with her gun drawn.

"Do you have to come behind me with that thing?" Lynn asked.

On the all-clear signal, a whistle from all girls, they met in the living room. Josie did a quick walk about

"She thinks we can't do anything," sniped Bettie.

"This is good, let's check out the two houses next door," Josie said.

They exited the house as Bettie muttered, "She can check them out herself."

They creeped next door. A cat ran out, spooking the women before scurrying into the bushes. As they entered the house the odour of urine and feces assaulted their noses.

"It stinks," Bettie said.

"It's only from the cat left locked in the house, "Katie said. "It had to pee somewhere."

The house was empty. After repeating the routine on the third house, the women picked the middle house for their night base. Josie drove the car over and parked it on the side of the house away from the road, under the shade of a large oak tree.

They checked out the cupboards. Two bottles of wine, some pork and beans, a can of corn and two cans of peaches. They found half a dozen full water bottles in the broom closet. They were in heaven: out of the car, relatively safe and sound, with full tummies. They hunkered down for the night. It was their first day out and everyone was still a little nervous. They posted a watch, two on and two off. The night passed uneventfully.

Chapter 10

After two days, the four still had not seen anyone. They did hear the same noises, gunshots and dogs barking, periodically. They were all on edge. It was like the whole world disappeared. An overripe smell hung in the air, more noticeable when they stopped. Up ahead they saw buzzards circling. At the overpass, cars were jammed up— and every car contained bodies that had been in the sun for days. The smell was horrible as swarms of insects whirred about.

The women pulled their shirts over their faces as the flies attempted to enter noses and mouths. Lynn barfed on Josie's leg as she retched in gut-wrenching heaves. The putrid, foul smell was unavoidable. They ran back to the car.

Bettie stopped.

"I see movement, someone is still alive in that mess," she shouted, and ran back to the gruesome scene. She got down on her knees, then drew back in horror.

"Rats," she screamed, rushing back to join the others at the car.

They climbed into the car, waving flies away. Josie backed up and turned around to head to the last ramp. Josie asked Bettie to haul out the map and find an alternate route.

"No," Bettie yelled. "I'm not going, Josie, take us back to Port Charlotte!"

"Bettie, slow down, we have to get out of this mess, hand the map to Katie."

"I don't care, you are trying to kill us," Bettie said. "You don't know anything."

Lynn sided with Bettie. "Josie, what are you doing?"

The disagreement heated up as Katie came to Josie's defense. Josie nodded, not quite trusting herself to speak.

The girls are actively hostile to me, Josie thought. But I know I'm not irresponsible.

"I'm only human and I'm trying my best," she snapped.

The argument petered out and the women drove on in tense silence.

They drove back along 1-75 about fifteen miles in dead silence. They were scared. The road looked clear, but they expected something to jump out at any moment.

After leaving the highway, the women grew calmer. Katie broke the silence.

"If we follow this road through two towns we'll bypass that exit and come to another exit."

They drove thirty miles through the two towns, which appeared to be completely abandoned. Swirling bands of colourful clothing moved in the vacant road. Suddenly Katie whispered, "Hey, look, up ahead. What do you see?"

They all saw a line of three people. Moods changed, and hearts became lighter.

"We're saved!" Bettie squealed.

"Oh my god, we are not alone," whispered Katie. Eyes sparkling with hope, they stepped out of the car.

Lynn's mouth fell open as tears glittered in her eyes. "It's a miracle."

The women creeped towards the three people. They stopped about twenty feet in front of the trio,

It was so quiet that Josie could hear the girls breathing. The wind picked up a little, dust swirled on the side of the road. The sun beamed down from a blue cloudless shy. There were two women, heads hung low, with tangled hair and scruffy, bruised arms. Their hands were tied together with electrical cord. As the four women moved closer they noticed crusted sores on the captive women. They were bound together by a thin rope around their necks.

A sinister, angry man of unknown age held the rope. He smiled.

"Hi girls, my name is Lord Scotty," he cheerfully uttered. His voice sounded too cheerful and phony, Josie thought. The tall, lean man sported dirty brown wrinkled pants, a sweat-soaked dark T-shirt and heavy army boots. Ropes of gold chain rested on his chest and he wore a huge diamond pinkie ring on each hand. His beady eyes, beneath a head of dirty, greasy hair, watched the four friends like a hawk.

Josie's right hand sneaked into her tote bag and cradled her pistol.

"Why the bonds?" she asked.

"I told you to call me Lord Scotty." He smiled cruelly. "They would run away."

The bound women did not speak. Their heads remained hanging down, but their eyes peeked up with hope.

"Girls, sit, join us," Lord Scotty said. "Tell me, what have you seen... are there others?"

"Nobody alive for the past two weeks or more, piles of dead people," Bettie blurted out.

Josie gave Bettie the look.

"Bettie, shut up," she whispered out of the side of her mouth.

"Don't tell me what to say," Bettie snapped.

Lord Scotty sidled up to Bettie, holding out his right hand. "I'll look after you, my beauty."

"Bettie, move away," Josie warned.

"I don't have too, Lord Scotty is going to look after me," Bettie said. "And he'll do a better job than you have."

Josie moved a little to the right and put a bullet between the despicable creature's eyes. "You deserve to die, you foul piece of shit."

As he fell to the pavement, Bettie screamed.

"What have you done?" she cried. "He was here to save us."

"He would not have saved you," said one of the bound women in a dry voice. "He would have made you part of his harem and raped you."

The friends stepped closer to the women and untied the ropes. The two freed captives burst into tears, grabbing their rescuers and thanking them through the tears.

The two women were sisters. Sandra, the tall thin one, cradled her sister, Maggie, who was pregnant, very pregnant.

The friends gawked at Maggie in awe.

Lynn stepped in to embrace Maggie.

"Your baby, when is it due?" she asked.

"I have no idea of the time," Maggie sobbed. "I don't know if it's Monday or Saturday. It's due in July, late July. I'm so scared."

The four friends huddled with the freed women, oozing gentle feelings and soft words to calm their new companions

* * *

Back at the car, they made room for everyone. It was a tight squeeze, but all were happy. Happy but dirty. They were all in need of major clean up. The four friends stank of sour vomit and Sandra and Maggie had sickening body odours. The whole car reeked. The women lowered every window in the car as they drove off.

About ten minutes they came to a sign marking an entrance ramp onto 1-75. Travelling another quarter mile, they arrived at a deserted oasis containing a trashed convenience store and gas pumps with empty cars lined up out to the road. They saw a Comfort Inn and pulled into a parking lot filled with dry debris, discarded food wrappers, and empty plastic bottles. Broken windows reflected the lowering sun.

A reeking fly-covered body propped up the sliding door. Katie and Lynn covered their faces with their shirts and grabbed plastic gloves from their backpacks. They dragged the corpse away from the door. Sandra propped open the door with a backpack.

Josie drew her pistol and motioned the others to follow.

"Do you have another gun?" Sandra spoke up. "I know how to handle one."

Josie thought about it for a moment. Then she opened the trunk and reached along the right side to pull out a loaded Glock.

They entered the building, Josie on the left and Sandra on the right, the others in line between them.

They did a quick search together, using the routine that Josie had taught them. They divided into two groups of three to search for water and food, always on guard for the unexpected.

As Katie and Sandra doubled back along the hall, they heard running water. Turning left through the swinging doors, they stepped into waterlogged carpeting. Excited, they almost ran past a door marked gym room. They looked through the glass—empty. Past two locked doors they squished down the hall. At the fourth door, they found the source of the flowing water. Sandra agreed to stay at the spot and Katie ran to the lobby yelling, "We found it, we found it."

The women converged on the hallway, splashing their way to the door. It was marked laundry room and it was locked. Josie aimed her gun, then reconsidered.

"Use this," Katie said, pulling an axe from a fire station near the end of the hallway.

Josie broke the door with a heavy ramming shot to the handle.

They stood transfixed; water poured from a broken hose. In a flash the women were stripping and dancing around in the water with cries of triumph and joy.

"Josie, come in, it's cold but it's heaven," Lynn called.

"I'm watching, standing on guard," she said. "I'll be in after you all. Keep the noise down."

They pulled soap and shampoo from one of the back packs and went to work. The women washed each other's backs, shampooed each other's hair, and giggled like girls at a slumber party, forgetting the harsh world.

After showering and drying, the women met in the breakfast room of the hotel. Katie wore funky plaid too-large man shorts with a cut-off pink top. Lynn looked outlandish in a neon-green skirt and red sparkly T-shirt. The rest were dressed in an assortment of odd, bizarre garments. Josie joined everyone in dry baggy brown clothes, carrying the axe.

Maggie fiddled with the light switch, shocking everyone when the lights came on.

Sandra glanced around the room, then located a closed door near the wall by the windows. "If I remember right this door should open into a storage area, where they keep the breakfast foods." She rattled the knob—locked. She glanced at Josie and winked.

Josie looked at the door, moved closer, and gave a mighty swing with her axe.

Wonders of wonders, rows of pine cupboards filled with food lined the room. Insects and vermin had destroyed all the fruits, cereal, and bread. But Sandra and Katie finally found eggs, bacon and frozen sausage patties in the freezer.

"Wow" Katie yelled, "I can make eggs."

Lynn said, "I'll fry up bacon and sausages."

The kitchen became an active beehive. Everyone laughed and worked together like a well-oiled machine. Later, with tummies full and bodies clean, the girls relaxed. Yawning and shifting in their seats, they all were soon ready for a nap. Sandra and Maggie left for a comfortable room they claimed.

"We have to talk about whether to take Sandra and Maggie with us," Josie said as the two women disappeared.

"What are you talking about?" Katie said. "We rescued them, and we care for them, we're family."

"We have to think of our resources, the size of the vehicle," said Josie.

"Josie, you selfish bitch!" screamed Lynn

"Are you going to give them your food, Lynn?" Josie asked.

"Josie, everything is always your way, you're nothing but a controlling son of a bitch," Bettie added.

Josie bit her lip.

"Let's sleep on it."

Chapter 11

Josie paced the bedroom floor, thinking she had really messed up. Josie was scared—if she showed weakness, the girls would leave. But she realized she had been ordering everyone around like they were soldiers in the army. Maybe she could lighten up a bit. After hours of restless pacing and heavy thinking, Josie realized that she had to be humble and listen, instead of solely giving orders. After all, her companions were mature women stuck in the same rotten situation.

In the morning, Josie faced a wall of hostile faces as the girls made their breakfast.

"Ah, hum, I just want to say I'm sorry," Josie said into the wall of silence. "My big mouth gets in the way."

"You got that right," Bettie sniped.

"Yes, well, I am what I am," Josie said. "It's how I was raised. My father was strict. I worshipped him, always doing my best at the shooting range, camping out, backpacking, you name it. I could not ever show weakness. I think I can use those skills to get us home. But you're all mature women, not girls, and I have to stop being so bossy."

She saw several smiles appear as she continued. "I'll seek advice from you all; if I become testy, please speak up. I'm afraid of being weak in your eyes and sometimes that makes me testy."

Her honest self-admission swayed several of the women. Katie was about to cry.

"I want to listen to your comments and most important, your feelings," Josie said. "It's just important to look after ourselves."

Bettie would not let her up easy. "Josie, you have been plain mean."

"I am sorry. Please help me be a better person."

The girls stood and began hugging Josie.

"Thank you for being honest," Lynn said. "We talked over our situation. I want you to know, Sandra is a third-year medical student, we want her. And Maggie is pregnant, close to time, we need to look after her, she's family."

"I thought about how crowded the car was, there is no reason why we can't squeeze in until we find a larger vehicle or take two cars," Josie said. "I was afraid that I couldn't save you all, but I see now we are going to save each other."

***

They cooked up more scrambled eggs and bacon, then put them in plastic containers then into a large tote box. Everyone soaked up more food, trying to use resources before getting into the supplies.

Maggie and Sandra found a Ford pick-up with a back seat and a long box. And the keys were in the ignition, an invitation to take it.

Sandra drove up beside the Venza and honked the horn. Josie instantly opened her mouth to ask her to keep it down—the sound might attract unwelcome guests—but then remembered her soul-searching breakfast speech and shut up.

The girls quickly transferred all the goods from the SUV to the back of the Ford. Josie looked up and saw Katie and Lynn stumbling through the hotel doors carrying armchairs amid hoots and laughs. Another chair came out under the swaying bodies of Sandra and Bettie. They loaded them into the open box of the pickup.

Josie thought a moment about leaving her car. But in the scheme of things, what was a car when compared with true friends. It was an easy trade.

They all trooped back into the hotel and looted the kitchenette of all its bottles of water and sealed large containers of juice. Cans of ginger ale were found and quickly loaded. Pillows and blankets were carted out, enough for everyone.

"Hey, we think we got it made," Josie said. Before they left, she drew a red maple leaf on the sidewalk.

* * *

The women decided to take a quick tour of the town in search of goodies. They passed an intersection where the traffic signals were out and turned right into a small mall of five businesses; a pharmacy, dry cleaner's, hair salon, store front proclaiming a massage parlour and real estate office. The pharmacy looked promising. They tried the door, but it was locked. They piled into their vehicles and drove behind the mall, thinking access would be more promising

No such luck. Josie retrieved her axe from the back of the truck. As she turned towards the door she saw a slight movement near the big green industrial waste bin. She raised the axe and peered closer. A young boy was huddled near a garbage bin.

Josie gently nudged him her left foot. He stirred; he appeared to be sleeping. The boy's clothes are slightly burnt, and some bare flesh showed, raw and red. Josie smelled smoke.

Suddenly he opened his bloodshot eyes. He stared at the women, all of whom save Josie stepped back. Josie lifted him in her arms; The odour of smoke and burnt flesh surrounded them.

"Careful, Josie, careful he's in shock!" Sandra shouted.

As Josie turned toward the girls she saw another child twisted in a pretzel shape and covered in soot. Josie placed the burnt boy into Sandra's arms, leaned down and rescued the second youth.

Sandra briskly accessed the children, then set up a drip feed from supplies found in the pharmacy. After she painfully removed clothing from the first boy's body, she applied a soothing antibiotic burn lotion to their bodies. Some wounds were so bad that she had to soak them with a saline solution. The older boy screamed out, then whimpered when she moved his right arm. Sandra noticed that his collar bone was broken.

They all stared in a muted horror.

"I don't want to move him. Katie, hold his wrist and pull when I tell you," Sandra said. "I feel the fracture, and when it is lined up properly we will wrap it into these bed sheets. Tear them into strips."

Katie gently did what she was told. The boy screamed, then lapsed into unconsciousness as Sandra set the break. She slid a sling on the boy while Katie kept him still. Then Sandra gave him a painkiller.

"The boys are very young, about eight and five years old," Lynn said. "What possible circumstance has brought this horrific condition?".

"My name is Sammy, and this is my brother Jerome," the older boy said. "I'll tell you what happened to us."

They all gathered around.

"We were in The Chapel of the Holy One," Sammy said. "My mom told us, 'Quiet, my sweet boys, this is the judgement I think.' Wow, the only time Mom called us 'my sweet boys' was when something bad was going to happen."

"The pastor sprinkled holy water all over himself and passed full jugs to the congregation, telling us to do the same. He shouted our scripture, repeating that God left us behind."

"'For our failed faith, we have been left here,' the pastor said. 'We must make a path to God. We can share this journey together, come everyone, and kneel in prayer.'

"One old man sitting right in the front of me sprinkled himself and his seatmate. Then he drank some of the holy water. It smelled like moonshine, just like Dad drank every night—he left a long time ago."

Sammy paused for a moment, then continued his story.

"The holy water splashed on me and when I smelled it again, I knew something funny was going on. Some of my best buddies were not in church, but their moms and dads were. Old man Edwards turned to me, winked and said, 'God is good!'

"I turned in my seat and saw two elders blocking the front door by putting a long two by four through the handles. It made me nervous; they had never done that before. I shook my mom's arm and told her I had to go pee. She told me to take my brother with me and come right back."

"As Jerome and I left the pew. Pastor Mike in flowing black robes, walked up to the altar. I saw him holler, 'God has left us behind, He thought us worthless, let's praise him, honour him by joining Him through death. God, we your humble servants are here on bended knees, ready to start our journey to meet you!'"

Sammy stopped and started crying as he came to the worst part of his story.

"Then he put a candle to his robes and whoosh! There was a big burst of red flame, a loud crackling sound, then a fireball explosion."

The women looked at each other in horror.

"It touched me, and I lit up. It hurt so bad. I ran to the bathroom with flames burning brighter. I got Jerome into the bathroom, closed the door and rolled on the floor to put out the flames, the way Fireman Al the Children's Pal said you should do. Then I boosted Jerome up onto the window sill and opened the window, I threw him out the window. I got out too and dragged him across the lawn to the edge of the road. The church just burned up," He shook his head. "It was like, like a volcano."

Sammy looked at the women, his bloodshot eyes shifting from one person to another, all strangers to him. "Mom, mom, they're all gone."

"We'll look after you and your brother," cooed Sandra. The women comforted Sammy, then placed him in a makeshift bed in the back of the truck. His brother, Jerome, curled up with Lynn in one of the stuffed armchairs in the bed of the truck.

* * *

They started out towards 1-75, robbing houses of food supplies. They skirted Lake City. The stink was awful, the dreadful smell of death.

Maggie was sitting up front with Josie, who explained her plan of finding a cottage in the country. They talked of home, and their concern that if they didn't reach the north by winter, they could be stuck because the roads would become impossible if snow moved in.

"I want a safe place for the birth of my baby," Maggie said.

Josie nodded as she checked the instrument panel. "We are low on gas."

"I know how to turn the pumps on manually," Maggie said. "I worked at the Racetrack gas back in Granville for three years. If the electricity is out sometimes there is a small back-up generator I can start."

As they rode past empty pasture, the hum of the engine was more noticeable with the quiet of the world around them. The highway was empty of people area six to ten vehicle pulled along the median, other area, empty.

What do we do? Josie thought. Can we continue on? So, there is hope up ahead?

Driving across the Georgia/Florida state border, Josie asked the girls to stop. As they rested by the roadside, Josie used the red soil of Georgia and handfuls of white stones to create a huge red maple leaf on the slope alongside the road.

"What's that for?" Bettie asked.

"Just to let other snowbirds know we're out here," Josie said. She thought about another maple leaf, the pin she had given to Clint. Oh, how she wished her P.I. with the yacht and the smooth moves was by her side.

"Josie, Josie."

Katie's incessant calling of her name snapped Josie out of her reverie.

"Josie, it looks like rain."

"Okay," Josie said, coming back to the here and now. "We should seek out the first trailer park and see if we can find some food and water. Having to use our backpacks should be the last resort. Katie, look there, that huge tent. It's what we need."

"Need, need for what?" Bettie asked, "Are you thinking of camping here? I would think, a trailer or two would be more suited for our needs."

"No, we can haul it down and rebuild on the back of the truck making a shelter."

Josie got everyone except the young kids to help tear the tent down, being careful to coil rope in one area, pile pegs in another, and place the central poles on the side next to some palm trees. It was a chore; the women got themselves tangled in the volume of canvas. After a few minutes of laughter, they were able to lay the tent out flat.

They placed poles in slots along the truck bed, ran ropes across the width of the truck, then fastened the assembly tight around the poles.

They lifted the corners but lacked the height to raise the center pole.

"Let's get some of those picnic tables and use those to get up higher," Lynn said.

"Thanks Lynn, that might work," Josie said. "Great idea!"

It took almost an hour to get things in place, but Lynn's idea worked like a charm. They backed off and stared at their work, proud of the venture.

They carried the last picnic table away from the truck and loaded their belongings. Setting out an assortment of foods on the table, they treated themselves to a smorgasbord of the supplies.

After the mixed meal of potato chips, peanut butter on crackers, some peas and corn, chocolate bars, cookies and beer, they sat together, resting and feeling pleased with themselves for making it so far together.

"Look, there's a small dog," Katie said to Bettie.

"Here puppy," Bettie said. "Are you hungry? Come girl, come."

The dog approached the gang cautiously sniffing with nose high in the air. Another dog, scruffy, lean and hungry-looking joined the first. The rest of the group noticed them.

"Come my pets, I'll feed you," Bettie said.

"Bettie, don't encourage them," Josie said.

"Here we go again, telling me what to do," Bettie said. Then she stood and shouted at Josie, "Don't tell me what to do! You agreed to be less bossy."

A half a dozen dogs of mixed breeds slithered out from the woods, not a sound among them.

Fear froze the women.

Bettie stood and waved her hands.

"Looks they're lonely, we can love them!" she said.

Seeing the slight movement, the dogs advanced steadily by small, slow steps. The women looked from Bettie to Josie, hopeful that someone would do something. Josie reached for her gun, but her tote bag was not there beside her. How could she be so stupid? She glanced around, there it was, three feet on her right.

"Everyone," Josie said in a soft voice. "Listen up, quiet-like. Stand slowly and get on the picnic table."

As they all stood in union, Josie leapt to the right, slid a body length across the grass, and reached for her bag. She rolled over with the gun in her hand. The dogs savagely snarled; their fur rose along their spines as their eyes tracked the girls.

"Up, now, up on the picnic table," Josie yelled, then fired. Two wild dogs ran off. Four dog bodies lay on the ground, but Katie lay among them.

The girls were petrified. Several collapsed into a huddle. Josie ran to check on Katie. Slipping and sliding through splattered gore, warm blood and dead bodies. She grabbed Katie, hauled her up, and checked her over,

"My arm," Katie moaned. Katie stares at Josie, "my arm." Her left arm seeped blood from a three-inch gash between her wrist and elbow,

Sandra ripped off her shirt to use as a bandage. She grabbed Katie's arm, then applied pressure to the wound.

"Someone grab my first-aid kit on the back seat," she yelled.

She led Kate to the table and asked her to sit. With medical kit in hand, Sandra poured alcohol over the open break in the skin. Then she bound Katie's arm.

"Drink it all Katie, it's for healing purposes," she said as she handed the woman a cup full of brandy. Sandra rummaged through her first aid kit and found a vial containing an anti-tetanus solution.

"This will only hurt a minute," she said, then injected the serum into Katie's upper left arm.

Chapter 12

After the wild dog attack, the party was happy with the monotony of their journey through a land without people. The girls settled down. The boys' wounds began to heal, and with the resilience of youth, they were soon happy, alert, and vying for the attention of the women. Katie's arm soon healed. The challenge soon became an old one—finding food and resources.

The crew found many houses and convenience stores which had already been looted. They began checking parked cars, keeping their distance from urban areas.

Everywhere there is the unbelievable stench of dead and rotting vegetation. Every breeze carried with it the stench of decaying cities. They wormed their way past wrecked cars and deceased people. Turkey vultures and crows fought for festering scraps of human and animal remains.

The women stayed on I-75, leaving the freeway only to check gas stations and convenience stores for supplies.

"Look - a Walmart sign, next exit, seven miles," Maggie shouted.

"What do you guys think?" Josie shouted.

"It's right down near the exit, Josie, we can't lose," Katie said.

Josie turned right onto the ramp, then up the incline to an intersection.

"There it is," shouted Bettie as the superstore hove into view.

At a reduced speed, Josie glided into the parking lot and stopped some distance from the store. She saw a line of cars clustered at the front entrance of the huge building.

"Lynn, please climb on the roof and check with the binoculars," Josie asked.

A moment later Lynn spoke up.

"Josie, check this out."

Josie climbed onto the roof and borrowed the binoculars. In front of the store sat a squat army tank and three army jeeps mounted with heavy guns manned by camouflaged men.

"Josie, it looks like an armed camp," Lynn said. Josie pointed the binoculars at the roof and discovered two men pointing at them.

"This is a war zone, some mean thugs have taken over the store and are protecting it, with battle prepared weapons. We are out of luck."

A rough grinding sound came from the parking jeeps as an engine turned over. A group of hard-assed, seasoned thugs ran out of the door and jumped into the jeep.

"Get in the truck, fast," Josie screamed to Lynn. She jumped off the roof, yanked the driver's door open and bounced onto the seat, Lynn was barely into the truck when Josie reversed it and backed out towards the road. She turned the truck in a tight circle and headed down the up ramp hoping to fool them. She pushed the truck to sixty, then seventy.

She narrowly avoided a parked car but scared the hell out of everyone when she smacked against a red car in the way.

Everyone was screaming. Those in the back under the tent were bouncing to and fro.

"Hang on, grab something, protect the boys, we are being chased by BAD, BAD men," Josie yelled. She passed an exit, slowed down, reversed, then speeded up on the on ramp. She slammed on the brakes. The truck made a series of spins.

The passengers screamed as Josie said under her breath, "Oh my gosh, I'm going to kill everyone." She slowed the truck down. She was shaking, and tried to concentrate amid the moans, groans, and screams from the unhappy group. She hit the gas again and headed right, then slammed on the brakes as she almost smashed into a roadblock.

She reversed, then headed left across the overpass. Passing an antique warehouse, she slammed on the brakes, turned, and drove into the empty parking lot, then drove around the side of the rust-red board building to hide the vehicle. Josie shut the truck off and sat there, head pounding.

"Shhh," she whispered to her stunned passengers. They all listened for sounds of anything. Josie heard only heavy breathing and whispered prayers. They sat and waited and waited. A shape crossed in front of the truck, causing everyone to shutter in fear. It was a deer. They relaxed a tiny bit.

Josie stepped down from the truck with sweat dripping off her face. She signaled the girls to be quiet.

"Lynn come with me, we are checking out this building."

They double-checked the road as they rounded the wooden structure. They slid up to the wide white door. It was locked. They walked carefully back to the truck, glancing back. Past the truck, she waved to the girls to stay. Josie stopped for a second to reassure the group in the back. They crossed to the back of the building and tested the door. Locked. Josie picked up a fist-sized stone and smashed down on the door handle half a dozen times. It sprung open. No alarms.

Lynn reached around the doorframe for a light switch, then found it—no lights. The building felt and sounded empty. The only light was from the front window. Josie and Lynn returned to the truck to reassure their friends.

"Just a little while longer," Lynn said.

She and Josie went back to the truck and rummaged through their packs for flashlights. With her pistol in her right hand, flashlight in her left, Josie led Lynn back into the building to case the joint. It was huge, loaded with carpets of all sizes, in piles here and there. The women's footsteps echoed on the hardwood floor. They made a full circle, then returned to the truck.

"Lynn, get everyone inside," Josie whispered. "I'm going to check out the road."

The road was clear, but the military guys haunted Josie.

"Lynn, help Bettie get some rugs outside and cover the truck. Katie and Sandra come with me, have to cover the windows with rugs."

66

With the building totally dark, Maggie found lots of kerosene lamps, some with fuel and several bottles and cans of kerosene. She lit two lamps. Everyone gathered around the light as Maggie showed them how to fill the base of the lamp, move the strips of webbing up or down with a turn of the little screw on the side of the lantern, then how to light it and make it brighter.

They checked out more of the building, barricading the front and back door to create a great fort.

They found a lunchroom containing one table, four chairs, a couch, and a vending machine, loaded. They targeted that machine in joyous emotion, thinking of those chocolate bars, bags of candy, and all that soda.

Josie retrieved her axe from the truck and smashed the machine open. They ate their fill, then loaded their backpacks. Sandra found some plastic shopping bags, Maggie and each of the boys filled them. The boys' eyes shined with wonder. Sandra cautioned them to only eat two chocolate bars.

After four days of rain, tensions rose, in part because they were bored. Nattering at each other led small disagreements grow larger. Josie decided that maybe it was time to see what was outside—if anything, the distraction might ease the ill feeling building up in the enclosed hideout.

Besides, the food was gone, so were the supplies from their backpacks and most of the stores from the truck.

Josie gathered the girls together to remove the barrier.

"I can help, I can, Josie," said Sammy as he jumped with excitement. "Let me, please let me." Many hands make light work, Josie thought as she smiled at the eager boy.

"Yes, Sammy I really need your help." As they worked at the barrier, Josie noticed Bettie reclining on a pile of carpets.

"Bettie!"

"I'm too tired and hungry," Bettie whined. "Josie, you've led us to a bad place again. You probably have a stash someplace, letting us starve."

Josie blocked out her words. Instead she lifted the edge of the rug covering the bathroom window. It had stopped raining. They removed the barricade to slide the door open a few inches. Katie pointed with excitement at several large, plump, bushy-tailed squirrels at play on a picnic table.

Food? Josie thought. How?

"I remember Dad teaching us how to catch a squirrel," she said to Katie. "But that was him, this is me."

"Let's see what we can find that'll help us," Lynn said. They searched the building, up one aisle down another.

"I don't know what I'm looking for, but I will know when I see it," Lynn said.

"There, a fishing net on a long handle, it's exactly what I need," Josie exclaimed.

"I'm with you, Josie, let's go big-game hunting," joked Katie.

They walked outside and creeped around the building, no noise. The men chasing them appeared to be long gone.

"Okay, Lynn," Josie said, "here's what we'll do." She laid out her plan, got some input from Lynn, then went to work.

Lynn placed a couple of chocolate wrappers on the picnic table, then anchored them down with a few stones. Meanwhile Josie took up a position four feet from the table, holding the fish net, motionless. She wanted to shift her feet, but she didn't.

Here they come, she thought, three frisky bundles of fur. They stood on their hind legs, noses quivering in the air. Josie waited, her heart slowed, and her body calmed down even as her mind raced a mile a minute. Was she downwind? No idea. She couldn't feel any breeze, if they caught a whiff of her they'd be gone.

With a leap the rodents were on the table, close together, sniffing at the candy wrappers. Josie took a quiet, slow breath, then brought the net down with a force so loud she heard it bang the table like a kettle drum. She looked.

"Two squirrels," Lynn exclaimed. They moved according to plan. She held open a thick industrial strength plastic bag the women had found, and Josie dumped their catch into the container. They sealed it shut, set the bag down, and waited.

"Now we have supper," Josie said. They left the bag on the table, waiting for the squirrels to suffocate.

"It may take a while," Lyn said, "let's check on the family." She liked to talk like that, imagining the band as a tight-knit family unit.

"Josie, these poor things, how could you do that?" carped Betty.

"It's food," Maggie said. "Bettie, you said you were hungry."

"It's okay," Sammy said. "I've seen my Uncle Larry hunt squirrels."

After a long wait of twenty minutes, Josie headed out the door with her backpack. She removed the animals from the bag. They were dead. Maggie pinned them to the table with a couple of nails through their furry legs, letting their bodies drop over the edge.

"Just like a dissection," Maggie said, as she expertly dressed the animals.

First, she removed their paws and tails, then she cut out the anus taking extra care not to get any feces on the meat. She pierced the skin at the neck, slipping her knife just under the skin in a line to the anus being careful not to puncture the intestines. She reached into the body and drew out the innards, then Maggie separated the heart and liver. She washed the carcasses with the last two bottles of water.

On the BBQ at the back door, Josie fired up a medium flame. She chopped the beasties into quarters and cooked them turning them regularly with her hunting knife.

Maggie scrounged some aluminum foil from the break room, which Josie used to cook the heart and liver. The smell was feral and meaty.

The girls hung around Josie as she cooked, their squeamishness evaporating as the food odours wafted over them.

"Supper is ready," she announced.

"Let's eat in the lunch room, we don't want to sit at the blood-stained picnic table," Katie said.

Josie loaded the hot meat on an open binder cover from the office and carried it into the lunch room. The women in their dirty clothes, their eyes looking out from their grime-covered faces, sat around the table. Sammy and Jerome sat on Sandra and Katie's lap. They all watched Josie, expecting the best.

"This might not be the best, but it's food," Josie said. "When we are finished we are on the road, we are going to find food and shelter."

A cheer booms out. She placed the meat in the center of the table; the aroma swirled around. There was a pause before everyone reached in and grabbed a piece.

"I am not eating this," Bettie said, "its stringy and tough."

"It's burnt in places and raw in small pockets, but it smells good and I am hungry," replied Lynn as she tore into the flesh. "Good job, Josie."

They finished the last of the meal, sucking on the bones to make tummies a little fuller.

Sandra suggested that all should learn the use of weapons and a little bit about fighting before they resumed their journey. Josie agreed as she hunted up her backpack and removed two pistols and a box of ammo. She slipped carefully out of the back door, telling the girls to be on alert.

"Alert," Bettie, "what is alert?"

Lynn rolled her eyes. "Come on, Bettie, just be ready to let Josie back in."

While Josie was outside, Sandra got help from Maggie and Katie as she propped up framed pictures on pile of carpets.

Josie gathered the girls together, after cautioning Sammy and Jerome to stay in the lunchroom and not come out while guns are firing.

She assumed the isosceles shooting stance.

"We form a triangle with the right leg quartered back for balance, left knee flexed, slightly bent, two hands on the pistol," she said. "These Glocks have no safety, most guns do. Aim at your target, take a deep breath, calmly pull the trigger."

"I'm first, I can do this," Bettie said. "I've seen how they do it on TV." She stood straight, arm extended, her legs a few inches apart.

"Bettie..." Josie said.

"Leave me alone, I can do this," Bettie said as she raised the pistol with two hands up near her chest, aimed and fires.

Bang!

The recoil put her flat on her ass. She screamed in a mix of foreign sounds.

"Damn you help me, help me up," she screamed. Katie and Sandra grab each arm and lift and lift. Bettie weighed a ton. They lifted her about four inches off the floor and let her slip to the floor. Lynn and Katie reached in and with their help, Bettie was lifted from the floor onto her two feet.

"As you can see," Josie said, "that is not the way." They all snickered at Bettie, who could only glare in return.

"Next?" shouted Sandra.

Katie stepped up. Soon she and Maggie had both taken a half-dozen shots and appeared to have a feel for the weapon.

Josie put the weapons away and suggested they continue practice later. The room smelt of gunpowder and was smoky.

Sandra had also planned out a sort of obstacle course run through the building, with lanes on barriers made of carpet rolls.

The boys were ecstatic running up and down the aisle. Their enthusiasm buoyed up the others, except Bettie, who sulked in a corner.

Chapter 13

The next morning, Katie hummed Willie Nelson's "On the Road Again," as the group packed.

"We are ready to head out," she said.

Sandra and Maggie carried out several carpets which they placed on the metal floor in the bed on the truck. Happy to be on the road, all of them began thinking about the next challenge—finding food.

Traveling northbound up 1-75, they saw hundreds of empty cars partly blocking the first lane and the shoulder, as if they had been pulled over one by one by someone signaling them to stop. They searched cars and trucks for food. Josie smashed open several tractor trailers. They found treasures such as a case of water or a bottle or two of soda on the back seats.

Eventually they pulled off on a ramp, tired and in need of rest. The convenience store at the end of the off ramp had already been raided, but a rundown motel looked like a promising place to rest. They left Katie and Bettie to watch the truck and the two boys.

The rest of them searched the rundown hotel, no luck. Josie walked back to the truck.

"Get the boys back in the truck," Lynn said. "Nothing here worth staying for."

"You sure you want to go into a town?" asked Josie as Katie and Sandra urged her to take the next exit.

"I don't think it will be as bad as an urban center," Sandra said.

They headed into town with the desire and confidence of folks too hungry to care. They passed two blocks of abandoned office buildings with coloured signs proclaiming welcome. But the streets offered only a few swirling pieces of clothing in all shapes and colours. No cars were in sight. Their route took them into a residential area, devoid of people. They heard dogs barking somewhere around a corner, but after their last experience with canines the women had no desire to meet them.

Josie drove into a faded blue paved driveway, stopped and gazed at a huge grey-stone Victorian house with a wide white porch surrounded by a blaze of god and red flowers intermingled with lush hostas. The porch held several forest-green painted wicker chairs and a tea table. A dark green carpet covered the steps welcoming them. The wide oak door with brass fittings in the center between huge floor to ceiling colourful cathedral light glass windows.

They did their routine check. Sammy and Jerome watched the street. The women gave them strict orders to yell out real loud if they saw people, dogs, or cars, then to run as fast as they could into the house.

Katie and Lynn headed to the back door. Bettie and Sandra checked out the front door. Maggie stood on the porch doing backup for the boys. Josie did a sneak advance around the house checking over the dark, glossy green hedge surrounding the back lawn. The neighbours' houses were quiet. Both front and back doors were unlocked. The girls calmly slipped into the building.

They investigated the house. Passing through a highly-polished entrance hall, they saw a huge framed mirror on the right and a dark walnut bench beside a walnut coat tree. Katie and Lynn browsed through the ultra-modern white kitchen, opening cupboards here and there. Yes! Packaged food. They met in the enormous dining room with several thick Indian carpets.

Bettie and Sandra checked out the basement. It boasted a comfy carpet, rust-red paint job and a large screen TV. There was a large purple and blue powder room with fluffy white towels. A cold storage room containing forty to fifty bottles of wine. Shelves along one wall were filled with homemade jams and jellies along with many mason jars with peaches and pickles.

Maggie and Josie scouted out the upstairs. Climbing the highly polished oak staircase, they noted the family portraits on the wall. They walked through a bedroom with matching twin framed prints on peach/pink wallpaper. A cozy chair sat by the peach draped curtains on the window. They checked out a bedroom with soft sage green carpeting with a white painted sculpted headboard towering over a queen-sized bed covered with a white crocheted bedspread and matching white floor-to-ceiling drapes. The closet held dresses and suits.

The rest of the upstairs was clean. A door opened into an attic that contained trunks, dressers and hampers full of linens. No people or pets, dead or alive.

Everyone met again in the dining room. An arched wood casement floor to ceiling window let in lots of sunlight. A white brick fireplace faced a polished pine table surrounded by twelve wooden chairs. A huge white vase containing dead brown flowers was in the center of the table. Looking through the six-foot-wide arched doorway, they could see the elegant living room, with a white moulded framed fireplace that flanked by a white leather sofa, and two white arm chairs. A white piano was in the background.

The vote was unanimous to sit tight for a while. Josie moved the truck into the large two door garage, pulled the forest-green doors down and stepped outside the door. She waited under the old oak tree for ten minutes or so; the street looked and sounded safe. She entered the house through the kitchen and found the girls giggling as they crowded together, opening cupboards. They spilled piles of canned goods and assorted packages of crackers and cookies onto the table, joining cans of spam, tuna, and sandwiches. Bottles of water and a dozen bottles of wine join the party.

They spent two uneventful days enjoying lots of comfortable beds, food, and drink.

* * *

A few days later they reload their backpacks, stashed water and wine in the back of the truck and headed back to the exit joining 1-75 north. No gas at the exit. The fuel gauge was below three-quarter. Their last hope was siphoning gas from a vehicle on the road or, better yet, finding gas containers on another vehicle.

No cars, no gas! The truck traveled on its last drop of fuel before sputtering out. No one was happy. They reloaded what they could carry on their backs and started out on the empty highway with the sun high overhead.

They looked a sight, sunburned and windburned, dressed in odd bits of clothes with long sleeves and neck wrappings to guard against the sun's rays. And still they walked, continuing north to home.

For Josie, it was a time of introspection. Her shoulders felt as if they were holding lead shoulder pads; her hips hurt as if she had arthritis. Her knees felt ready for replacements and her feet screamed.

And yet another hill loomed. We have to find a car, truck or anything with wheels, Josie thought, we've only covered eight miles, based on the mile marker at the side of the interstate.

If I hurt, what about the others? She thought. She slowed, then paused and looked back. Her friends were stretched out for yards and yards.

"Where is Bettie, I cannot see her," Josie said as she wiped sweat from her face. "Rest break! Stay here in the shade along the fence, I'll be back."

Far down the road Josie saw a lump. As she got closer she could hear wailing. Bettie was slumped down, in a heap, motionless. Was she dead?

As I neared her, I heard her crying, deep sobs and cursing a blue streak.

"Bettie, how goes it?"

"Damn you Josie, this is utterly dumbass, you will kill us all," Bettie sobbed. "You just have it in for me, don't you?"

"No, Bettie, it's the luck of the draw, we are without wheels, that is tough but—"

Bettie erupted. "Tough? Tough your ass! Why did we have to leave the house? We had lots of food. You enjoy making me suffer!"

"Here, let me help you sit up." Josie tugged and tugged and finally hauled her into a sitting position. Her legs opened in front of her with her dress bunched up at her hips.

"Let me get you some water," Josie said. But there was no water left in Bettie's backpack, only a few knick-knacks.

"Bettie, you have no provisions."

"I drank and ate it all because there was only a little."

I reached into my pack and handed her a bottle of warm water, which she grabbed and guzzled in long swallows.

"Slow down, girl!" Josie pulled out a chocolate bar and was about to split it when Bettie grabbed the whole thing.

She ate it in two bites.

"Bettie, we need to join the others, they are about ten to twenty minutes away. Come on."

Josie tried to chivvy Bettie along, but to no avail.

"Josie, find a car and come pick me up."

"Bettie, I can't do that right now. Come on, you can stand, I will help you. I will help you walk."

"Okay, but don't walk fast, I'm all sore on my inner thighs."

"Let me see," Josie said. "Yes, the skin is all blistered and red." She dug into her pack, found some Vaseline, and applied it to the raw area.

In an hour, they stumbled up the highway and joined the group. With a sigh of relief from everyone, the sun slid behind the clouds.

How come when we are in such physical pain there is not a car in sight? Josie thought. Thank goodness it had become cloudy.

They spread out on the pavement in a long file as they walked and walked. A slight breeze stirred the grass along the road; they were thankful. They stumbled along like snails, placing one foot in front of the other. Voices of discontentment stopped, there was dead silence with an occasional sigh or puff of heavy breathing. They plodded on and on and on.

Suddenly they drew abreast of a van, a delivery van. Rays of sunlight filtered through the clouds lighting up the slogan, a huge picture of tomatoes surrounded by different vegetables. Printed under the painting www.lordes.com. A smaller painting on the passenger door of a basket of green grapes, apples and strawberries was underlined with the slogan, "Quality of Life."

After a quick look through the windshield, Josie yanked the passenger door open. They were all surrounded by hordes of buzzing flies. They banged into faces, hit eyes, and went up noses and into ears. As the friends wiped their mouths and spit out dead flies, the swarm was up and gone. A rotten swampy smell followed their departure.

They gathered around the van muttering expressions of thankfulness. They quickly clean out the rotten veggies and the crawling maggots. The floor of the van was wet from the mess, so they stripped out the floor mat. Everyone piled into the back and helped Bettie in.

"Hey, we do not know if it will even run," Lynn said. She stepped out of the back and climbed into the driver's seat, where the keys were dangling from the ignition. She gave it a twist.

GR... unk. Gr... unk. A sigh breezed through the van. She gave it another go. It started, purring like an overgrown lion cub to the cheers of the footsore travelers.

Chapter 14

I'm tired, hungry, and not thinking straight, Josie thought. I'm thankful Lynn is driving, it leaves me time to think. My mind is blank. Has the sun roasted my brain?

They had traveled about 20 miles when a discussion about what to do next escalated into a loud argument. Near exit 39, the women agreed to take the ramp off the interstate.

"Where to?" Lynn asked. "Does anyone want to pick a hotel?"

"Why not the Super 8?" Katie said, "It's right in front of us."

"I agree," Josie said. "We're tired. Go for it, Lynn."

They pulled into the entrance and stopped at the main door. Within a blink of an eye, a big beefy guy with red and green tattoos outlined in black running from his wrist up to the edge of his clean white muscle shirt jumped in front of the vehicle. His buddies surrounded him. The men wore jeans, black biker boots, and sleeveless black T-shirts.

Belts of gun cartridges crisscrossed their chests. All of them watched with indifference, smoking stinky cigars, rifles held at rest.

"My name is Dale, I make the rules here," he said. "If you break the rules, you'll get the piss beat out of you. You are nothing, you sluts. You all belong to me. Do you understand?"

Dale cockily walked back and forth as the women were hustled out of the truck. He wore a pistol tucked into the front waistband of his jeans. His black leather kick-ass boots thumped on the ground. His head was shaved bald; a four-inch ragged scar was visible in the folds of skin on the back of his neck. A gold hoop dangled from his left ear and a gold ring shined on his nose.

As the women were marched through the open doors into the lobby Josie noticed huge black leather sofas and armchairs resting on layers of Turkish carpets. Under a mismatch of bright lamps, she saw large cushions scattered around spaced with African ornaments.

Lynn was separated from us.

Josie protested and was rewarded with a slap in the face. A short redheaded girl about twelve or thirteen escorted Lynn to a hallway. As she passed into the corridor, Lynn gave a small wave. Josie gave her a thumbs up. Two armed men follow them.

Lynn was taken into a large suite containing white leather couches and armchairs. Shiny glass end tables and coffee table filled the room. The armed men stepped into the room and stomped to a halt. Not a word was spoken by the redheaded girl.

Lynn started to complain, but the girl quieted her, shaking her head and pointing at the men. They passed through heavy wood sliding doors to a bedroom. A four-poster king-size bed covered with a variety of furs dominated the room.

As they entered a bathroom, mirrors reflected Lynn from the walls and ceiling. They revealed a scared, road-weary woman and a redheaded robot of a girl who guided Lynn towards a pink marble tub. Next to it was a long pink marble vanity covered with an assortment of creams and lotions. Lynn stumbled a bit when the girl let go of her arm.

"My name is Pet, some call me Pretty Pet. I'm going to help you bathe and dress."

"What about my friends?"

"They will be looked after. Here, drink this cold juice."

Within minutes, Lynn was stripped and settled in the whirlpool tub. She was bathed and perfumed; her hair was dried as it curled into long ringlets pinned back from her face with lacquer pink pins. A pink negligee was placed over her head, floating down her body to conform to her curves.

Pet walked Lynn to the king-size bed and handcuffed her to the top right post.

"The boss will be in soon," she said, then left the room.

After a soundless hour or more, Lynn slowly recovered her wits. She had been drugged. And the worst was yet to come.

The room's door opened and closed with barely a sound. Dale marched into the bedroom, smiling. He removed his gun, and then rapidly removed his clothing.

He stood admiring his tan muscular build in the surrounding mirror. Sliding his hand across the back of his bald head, he climbed onto the furs covering the bed. Without talking, he forced himself on Lynn.

* * *

Time crept by as Lynn's friends sat on the leather sofa in the lobby, eyeing each other with a tiny shrug here and there. Josie glanced at the two unsavory men pacing in a cocky ramble around the perimeter, high fiving each other as they met. The two men were so intent on their own importance, they hardly ever looked towards their unwilling guests.

"Enough is enough" Josie whispered, thoughts of how to rescue Lynn running through her head.

Following the movement of their guards, Josie saw the redheaded girl. She walked boldly into the room and addressed the guards.

"Hey, shouldn't you guys be making supper or something?"

"Hey, you're right," said the smaller man. "I'm hungry."

"What about them?" asked the other guard, looking at the captive women.,

Hey, what about them?" answered the girl. "The doors are locked. The other guys are patrolling the outside."

"Ok, let's get us some grub," they said as they trotted towards the breakfast room.

The young girl motioned Josie to slip into the hall. The others sat rigid in their seats.

"Relax, be quiet," Josie said to her companions as she left the room.

"Come, your friend is three doors down; I have the keys to her handcuffs," the girl said.

"Handcuffs?"

"You don't want to know!"

Josie entered the suite, her mouth dry with fear.

Pet unlocked the cuffs. Lynn grabbed Josie, sobbing. As Josie looked into the humiliated, angry eyes of her friend, Lynn gripped her shoulder.

"Josie, get me a gun!"

Pet opened the door, then peeked up and down the hall. "It looks safe, hurry! hurry!"

She ushered them out of the room, down the hail to the right, then pointed to the exit door.

"I'll get your friends, hide in the bushes."

Pet slid into the lobby, motioning to the gang to stay quiet. Then she yelled out to the guards. "I'm taking the prisoners for a pee break."

The guards didn't care; they were intent on stuffing their faces.

Everyone stood and moved with tensed muscles down the empty hall out an exit door.

They gathered in a flower bed, reaching out to touch each other with silent promises to get out, stay together, and get as far away as possible.

They slipped along the building, huddled together. There was their vehicle, right where they left it. Pausing every dozen step or so, checking, checking, they sneaked past the front entrance. Silent prayers were whispered as they slowly opened the door and entered. Josie slid into the driver's seat and reached for the keys that were left there.

Chapter 15

As Josie travelled north, she pondered the past, the end of civilization, and meeting her newfound love, Clint. Where was he? Would she ever see him again? About the present, we been through the good, the bad and the ugly, she thought. For the future, it is one step then another towards safety. I must keep positive.

Meanwhile, Clint was searching for Josie. He was on her trail. The stink of rotting bodies was detected as soon as he entered the driveway of Josie's home in Port Charlotte. His heart slowed in fear. He checked out the street, empty except a few scattered piles of clothing, some wound around trees, lots piled against parked cars.

He parked his bike and turned towards the house. Tense, he eyed the door propped open by a rotting fly-blown corpse. Another one lay a few feet past the door.

He yelled, "Josie," upsetting the flies, who took flight. The house answered with silence and the flies settled back to their meal.

As his gaze traversed the room, Clint saw painted on the living room wall a large red maple leaf. Evidence showed that the girls had packed and hot-footed it out of there.

Clint touched the maple leaf pin Josie had given him, his mind made up. She would head north, he thought, so that's where I'm going too.

At the ramp on 1-75 pointing to 301 Zephyr Hills, something caught his eye, Clint stopped, climbed off his motorcycle, and walked towards a red maple leaf marked across a for sale sign. He gently touched it, the red lipstick that was used for the sign stuck to his fingers. He put his fingers to his lips.

"Josie," he said, and offered up a prayer of thanks and safety.

Further up 1-75 near the Georgia border, Clint faintly saw a huge Canadian flag fastened to the building. In his hurry to check it out, he didn't notice half a dozen people hiding around the parked cars.

He stopped and stared at the red maple leaf. He barely heard the people surrounding him.

"Get off your bike," a voice grated in his ears. "Remove all weapons, you know the drill, hands up, we have you covered."

Clint slid off his bike and deposited his gun on the ground.

"Now, who are you?" a woman asked. "And why are you interested in this decoration?"

"I'm following the woman I love; she's with a group heading north."

Sally, a dark-haired Spanish woman who appeared to be the spokesperson, stared hard at Clinton, as if gauging his soul. After a long moment, she spoke.

"Pick up your gun," she said, as the tension seemed to lessen. "We're following a group of Canadian women with weapons, who know how, fighting their way north. We could use them. We've been protecting people and guiding people to safety."

A man in the group walked up and held out his hand.

"We're looking for a safe haven, following the red maple leaf, it's posted along 1-75 on convenience stores, gas bars and exit signs. All pointing north."

"Josie," Clint said. He had missed her by a few weeks.

* * *

The silence in the truck was deafening. Josie glanced around the interior.

"Hey everyone, we're on our way home," Lynn shouted.

At the on ramp to I-75, Josie stopped, sat for a few minutes, then got out of the truck.

"Why are we stopping?" whined Bettie.

"Come on, everybody, this will only take a minute," Josie said.

Soon the whole gang pitched in, hauling red soil from a nearby field, packing it together with water from a swale, and molding a huge red maple leaf.

"One more thing," said Katie, her mood improved by the activity. She grabbed a few bright articles of clothing strewn along the road and began creating a border around the maple leaf. Soon the others joined in, even Sammy and Jerome. They weighed down the border with gravel, then stepped back to admire their work.

In the heat of the morning, with the hot sun beating down, they stood before the symbol of hope and defiance they had created and thought their own thoughts, everyone silent with their thoughts.

"We've come a long way," Josie said, breaking the silence.

"Hey, we're on our way home!" sang out Lynn. The women and boys turned to each other, reached out, touched, and shares smiles of friendship.

Then it was back to the truck and on the road again.

There was a lot more chatter in the vehicle after the stop than there had been earlier. The crew passed numerous vehicles pulled over along the road. They stopped here and there, looting cars for any treasures. They found bottles of water, a box of cereal, unopened boxes of crackers, and lots of unopened bags of potato chips. They also grabbed odds and ends of clothing. Although they had loaded the truck with food and water, experience had taught them not to pass up a chance to stock up. The fear was there now, the fear of having no supplies.

About two miles past Cordelle, Georgia they stopped and stared. A bad pile up of vehicles blocked the highway.

"Would you look at that," Lynn said.

They got out of the truck for a closer look—there was no way through. The guard rail stopped them from driving over to the southbound lanes.

"We're going to have to take the back roads," Sharon said. She looked at Josie. Neither one of them relished the thought of abandoning the wide-open highway for desolate, hidden tree-bound lanes where ambushes could lurk.

But they had little choice. They climbed back into the truck, turned around, and headed back to the exit at Cordelle. Taking highway 280, they tacked north again towards Americus. They passed empty fields and came near a few cows and horses on the road that bolted and ran ahead of them.

They slowly moved towards Plains, home of President Jimmy Carter, a town reported to house about 700 people. It was an oasis of parks and recreational spots. Plains seemed like a good place to stop for the night.

They drove into Plains with the sun shining in their eyes.

"Wow," squealed Bettie. Out of the brightness along the buildings, dozens of people slowly milled around with beaming smiles on clean, shiny faces. People resting on park benches along the storefronts stood and moved with the crowd towards us. They were all waving at the travellers, clapping their hands, all swaying in rhythm, welcoming them with all smiles.

"This is weird, like the 'Stepford Wives' southern edition," Maggie said.

But Sammy noticed something even weirder.

"Where are the kids," he piped up. "Where are the boys and girls?"

"Maybe they're protected behind closed doors," Lynn said.

But Josie was already in alert mode.

"Roll up your windows," she snapped. "You guys in the back there, slip down onto the floor, keep your cool, and let me speak first."

An elderly woman wearing a clean pinkish dress held out her hand at Josie's window.

"Hi lady," she said, beaming. "We all welcome you, please come into the Mimmie Diner and feast with us, enjoy a cool lemonade."

Do I trust or not? Josie thought. Going with her gut feeling, she stepped out of the truck.

"Cover me," she said in a soft voice to Sandra. A path opened in front of Josie, leading towards the Mimmie Diner.

"I'm Ms. Harris, the mayor of beautiful Plains, welcome, welcome," said a soft-spoken plump 40ish woman. "We don't have visitors often, but we will treat you first-rate."

The crowd erupted in thunderous applause.

Ms. Harris guided me towards the restaurant. It looked clean. Josie looked up, casing the building and grounds for snipers or hidden threats. A pleasing whiff of roast pork hung in the air.

Josie signaled the group in the truck to join her. The crowd cheered, whistled, and applauded with delight as they ushered the women and boys out of the hot sunlight into the cool, semi-dark restaurant. They were shown to a long table made up of several smaller tables pushed together.

"Please be seated, y'all," Ms. Harris said. She turned to the kitchen area and said in a loud, cheery voice, "Bring out the best, you chefs, for our new friends."

As they settled into chairs at the table, there was a buzz of voices as plates and silverware were set in front of them and along the table.

Over a background of country and western music, Josie asked about the tunes.

"We have loads of batteries," Ms. Harris replied with smugness. "And listen to this; we've a working huge windmill to energize power for lights."

"Wow," Sandra spoke up. "How many are you?"

"Oh, maybe fifty or so," Ms. Harris purred. "Please, pour the wine."

As they sat chatting, someone pressed Josie's hand. When she turned, there was no one there, but in her hand was a scrap of paper.

"Don't eat the meat," was written on it in a shady script. Weird, thought Josie, but she decided to take no chances.

"Don't eat the meat," she whispered to Lynn. "Pass the word down to the others."

Platters of fresh-cooked bread appeared on the table. The aroma made Josie giddy with thoughts of home. Ms. Harris bowed her head.

"Bless our new friends, that we may enjoy them for a long time. Blessed are the chefs who made this bountiful meal. Bless this food to our bodies. Amen."

A line of wait staff carried trays of hot soup to the table. Every diner reached for a bowl. It smelled delicious with just the right blend of spices.

Josie placed the bowl in front of her and reached for the bread. The townspeople downed the soup in seconds and began sucking on bones.

"This is good," Bettie chortled as she swallowed a spoonful. The townspeople beamed as one.

Chatter picked up as Lynn, Katie and Josie consumed more bread. Josie took a closer look at her soup. There, floating to the surface, was a tiny finger!

No wonder these people are well fed, Josie thought with horror, they're cannibals! No wonder there are no children, they went into the soup pot first!

Josie looked around. The boys were hungry but had listened to them and were filling up on bread. No one was watching the companions, instead the townspeople were concentrating on their second helping of soup. Josie nudged Lynn with her elbow, as she dumped her soup between her legs onto the floor. She followed suit, helping the boys discard their soup. Maggie and Sandra looked to Josie for direction.

Josie stood up.

"Wait, wait, the main course is coming, y'all," shouted Ms. Harris.

Josie grinned and whispered to her, "The boys have to go to the restroom.

"Ah, oh, we'll begin," Ms. Harris said, "you'll join us when you can!"

Josie signaled Maggie with winks and shakes of her hand. She got it and whispered to Sandra. They took the boys towards the restroom. As they passed Josie she uttered under her breath, "Find a back door, take yourselves to the truck."

Lynn decided to go with the boys. Katie and Josie tried to get Bettie's attention, but her eyes were on the steaming trays of meat coming to the table.

Josie grabbed her wine glass and proposed a toast to the wonderful caring townspeople, especially to Ms. Harris for her warm welcome. She sipped at the glass, glanced at Bettie, then spilled the contents of her glass at her.

"Arrgh," Bettie moaned, as she stood and shook out her purple-splattered white top.

"Oops, oh, I'm so sorry, the glass slipped," Josie said. Some people turned to look at the commotion, but the platters of meat soon grabbed their attention again.

"We are out of here, danger girl, danger!" Josie whispered to Bettie.

But Bettie shook her head as the platters of meat were placed along the table. Instead, she reached for a hunk of roast meat. I shudder.

"Sorry Ms. Harris, I better check on the boys."

As Josie passed Bettie, she yanked her to her feet.

"What? What? Let go of me, you bossy bitch. Just as I'm about to get some real food—"

Josie silenced her with a quick jab to the ribs.

"Listen, fool, that's human meat—like people."

Bettie gagged and began dry-heaving.

"It's her ulcer again," Josie said to Ms. Harris, "I'll take care of it—I know just what to do."

What she wanted to do was punch Bettie in the face for allowing her greed to overcome her common sense and endanger the group.

But Josie kept it together as she helped Bettie to the restroom.

Ms. Harris and the townspeople were oblivious, in blessed bliss, humming over their meal. She barely looked up as Josie hustled Bettie down the hall, through the back-exit door, and onto the street. around the building heading towards the street.

Six skinny people stood there, gesturing towards Josie and Bettie. Beyond them, Sandra shrugged her shoulders as the rest of the travelers got into the truck.

One of the strangers motioned toward Josie to keep quiet, then the other five jumped into the crowded bed of the truck.

Lynn took the wheel and drove fast and sure, heading north until the town of Plains was no longer even a blur in the rear-view mirror.

"Let's pull over here," Josie said from the shotgun seat. "I think we should get acquainted with our new friends.

"Thank you for saving us," said an older man who introduced himself as Frank. "We're not sure if we could have held out much longer.

One by one the former Plains residents introduced themselves. They collectively told a story of a decent town that descended into cannibalism as conservative older townspeople grew desperate to survive.

"We are now a band united together for safety and looking desperately for shelter," Josie said. Her words were grim, but as everyone squeezed back into the van, they could only nod in agreement. Even Bettie, with visions of human roast still etched in her brain, did not answer back.

The day had moved along, the clock in the vehicle showed the time to be close to three p.m. Lynn, with Sandra and Josie navigating, had found her way back onto I-75, and the travelers were beginning to settle into the lulling monotony of long-distance travel.

The black, newly paved highway was empty, beckoning them onwards, but the smoke drifting in the wind reminded them all of death. They continued to avoid the towns and cities, thinking of the possibility of disease, flies, rats, mad dogs, and even madder humans.

"Look ahead, up there, what's that?" said Katie.

"It looks like a human chain across the road, from ditch to ditch," Maggie yelled from the rear.

Lynn came to a stop and looked, seeking a way back. Suddenly there were more voices as five or six people rose from the steep sides of the road from where they had been hiding in the swales.

Is this bad or what? Josie thought as she and Sandra reached for their weapons.

"Would you look at that?" Katie exclaimed. "There's every color of the rainbow out there."

Sure enough, the newcomers were people of every hue dressed in every outfit imaginable—a man in a wedding dress, a woman in a cowboy outfit, Batman and Wonder Woman, began waving and shouting at the truck.

Suddenly two people, a woman in a flowing Arabian outfit and a man in a tuxedo, came forward with their hands raised in peace.

"Josie?" Lynn asked.

"I'll take care of this," Josie said. "Keep the motor running, honey."

The travelers were dead silent as the hub-bub of voices decreased. There in the middle of the road near day's end, Josie met the delegation.

A middle-aged man with a scruffy dark beard carrying a backpack stepped towards Josie.

He wiped his dirty hands on his dirty jeans, then put out his arm to shake Josie's hand.

As politely as possible, Josie looked at the soiled hand reaching towards her and just waved.

"We don't mean to scare you," the man said. "We been walking for a week or more, seem to have lost the sense of time. We're heading south, where are you coming from?"

Josie spoke out louder than necessary so that everyone in the van could hear her.

"Whoa, slow down, let's talk. I'm Josie and you are?"

A tired young woman, maybe twenty-five or so, set her backpack down onto the road. She raised a bangle filled arm in the air.

"Hi, we just been walking and walking. It's lucky you have wheels. Oh, don't worry, we won't bother you, we're looking for shelter. It'll be dark soon."

"How many of you are there?"

The unkempt man smiled. "Eleven tired, hungry, and peaceful souls," he said.

"Walking to where?"

"My name is Fred," the man said. "This is Liz. Don't know where we're going, but we know what we're looking for. We're hoping to find good people, a compound, a safety zone, something."

Josie looked at the group and made a split decision.

"You can join us, it'll make it crowded, but we'll work it out, OK?"

Bettie moved up beside Josie and whispered, "Josie, are you nuts? They could be murderers or druggies robbing us, don't let a smiling hunk of a man shade your mind!"

Fred laughed, and Liz smiled.

"We may like a little herb," she said, "but Fred's no hunk and we mean you no harm."

Bettie was mortified; she didn't think the strangers had heard her disparage them.

"Bettie, they have their own food, they're not going to rob us."

Josie signaled Katie to come forward.

"Katie, check out the map, Byron should be around here, I thought I saw a route sign."

"Byron is at exit 148, we've just passed exit 146."

"Thanks Katie," Josie said.

"Fred, back towards the north is Byron, do you want to come with us and try to find a place for all of us?"

Fred agreed. By this time there was standing room only in the van. Besides, Lynn mentioned that the gas gauge was dropping dangerously close to E. Josie knew that with the sun going down, they needed to get somewhere safe to regroup.

At the exit sign for Byron, Lynn stopped the van. Everyone got off and began milling around. Katie, Josie, and Lynn pulled several cans of red paint from the van.

"What are they doing?" asked one of the newcomers.

"You'll see," spoke up little Sammy.

The women quickly painted a red maple leaf on the concrete of the overpass, a clear sign to anyone heading up I-75.

Just off the ramp the travellers found a burned-out filling station. Sandra used her skills to get a pump working and they were able to fill the van—one worry taken care of.

In better spirits, they drove on toward Byron. There was a faint odor of gas and smoke in the air, but no smell of dead bodies. They headed towards the city.

"Up there, see that big pale peach building with the big clock on the wall" Josie said as they rolled into Byron. "What is it?"

"I don't know, but guessing I would say a municipal building," Katie said.

Lynn steered left at the second intersection and drove up to a magnificent peach stucco three-story building. A wide ten-foot set of cement steps led up to wide hazel doors with highly polished handles, maybe brass.

The building looked deserted. Above the doors in white stone huge letters read, "Courthouse, Peach County."

Josie climbed the steps, looked back toward the street, then disappeared inside the unlocked building.

"She's nuts," Bettie said. "Who knows what could be hiding in there? And with these people..."

she looked around at the newcomers, who returned her look of disdain with dull, tired eyes.

Suddenly the door opened, and Josie stepped out. She waved to the group of misfits who began coming slowly up the steps towards her.

"Hey listen up. It's big and roomy; it'll hold all of us," Josie said. "It probably has a lunch room with vending machines, and maybe a cafeteria or storeroom containing food."

At the far entrance under a fan window, double doors lead into a big empty courtroom exactly like the ones seen on TV crime shows. It was dark in the room, but Josie could make out the witness box, the jury box, and the benches lined up from the doors to a wood gate, making a fifteen-foot space in front of the judge's desk.

They did find a lunch room on each floor holding vending machines full, yes full of sandwiches, chocolate bars and bags of chips, some cookies and Twinkies. The pop machine was full too—heaven!

Fred hollered up from what Josie assumed was the basement.

"Hey, I found a generator," he yelled in excitement. "I think I can rev it up!"

If that were not reason enough for joy, further discoveries made the decision to come to Byron seem even better.

The weary travellers found cases of water and pop, boxes containing bags of chips, pounds of candy bars. In the upper cabinet, they discovered tea and coffee, plus coffee filters, jars of powdered milk packets of sugar and bags of foam coffee cups.

On the counter was a coffee machine and an electric kettle.

They had everything except electricity.

Then without warning the lights flickered, then came on...and stayed on. The dull rumble from below meant Fred had managed to get the generator going.

Maggie reached over to the sink and turned the tap. Gurgle, gurgle, spit, spit, hiss, and then a slow steady flow of water. Cheers echoed through the hall.

Soon the group had a production line at the coffee machine and had set the tea kettle boiling. They all helped themselves to the bounty in the lunchrooms and, over food, barriers began to fall. Even Bettie, with crumbs falling from her blouse, was in a good mood.

The original group of travellers got to know their new friends. It had been a while since any of them had been with others who could tell stories back to them about the phenomenon that had left them all dazed and confused.

Fred and two other men from his group walked around locking doors and securing windows. Josie sat back, happy to see the job of security being undertaken by someone other than her.

Soon the disparate groups began picking rooms. Some chose to stay in the common area, on floors or sofas. Some camped on the floor, the lucky ones had claimed the sofas in waiting areas in some offices.

"I suggest we turn off the generator," Fred said. We don't need the light and it may advertise our presence."

"Good idea, Fred," Josie said.

But she still slept with her Glock nearby.

Chapter 16

The thrown-together travellers awoke to the mouth-watering smell of coffee brewing. A breakfast feast of crackers, peanut butter, jam and chocolate bars had been laid out by Liz, Katie and Bettie. The boys were in high spirits, caught up in a sugar rush and the joy that comes from being safe after living in fear.

Fred was absent, and Josie wondered about that briefly before partaking of the great breakfast. As she opened her mouth to take a big bite of a chocolate bar, a noise made her stop in mid-gulp.

A rough clanking sound filled the air. Josie turned in surprise, then beamed as she saw what greeted her.

Fred waved up at her from the driver's seat of a big yellow school bus as he parked it behind the truck that had brought them so far.

"Hey, everyone," he shouted, "Come on, your chariot awaits you!"

The large group poured out of the courthouse with raised voices, high fives, hugs and strains of joyous song. No discussion was needed; soon, there was a back and forth movement as individuals returned to the courthouse to fill backpacks with food. Soon a cheer rebounded in the loaded bus, "Go, bus driver, go!"

The merry group left Byron behind as the bus rocked with joyful songs not heard for a long time.

It wasn't a song sound exactly. It wasn't anything they could pick up with their ears. It was closer...already inside their heads. The sensation intensified, mounting, mounting. It felt like bugs swarming. The buzz, buzz; then, a purr.

First anger, then acceptance, and then the desire to please it. Josie recognized the buzz and jumped out of her seat.

"Hey people, people listen up, Start counting, let's count together."

The bus came to a jarring stop. Fred jumped out of the driver's seat and rushed out of the open door. Two young people ran off the bus, running ahead, shedding their clothes as they screamed with joy.

Josie and her friends followed, drawn by the buzz, buzz. The group stumbled to a halt in front of a tall man in a cloak. Well, he looked like a man, if a man could grow ten feet tall.

Josie yelled louder. At first her three friends remembered, and they began leading more of the group in chants of alphabets, numbers, and nursery rhymes to drown out the consuming buzz.

The man-thing stood before the humans, dressed in thick, wide black metallic boots, armed with a gun the likes of which Josie had never seen. A huge machete, curved like a scimitar, hung from a broad black belt.

It beckoned them closer, despite their chants. Its pinpoint yellow feral eyes watched them. Its mouth opened from ear to ear, revealing ridges of shiny sharp fangs damp with drool.

"We must be strong," Josie screamed as she felt the elemental evil of the thing. "Remember, count, damn it, count, your life depends on it."

A sonic wave pitched into Josie's brain, beaming what felt like a whole movie condensed in a few seconds. She saw a story about stragglers being rounded up by creatures like the one before her. They wanted people, lots of people, all who were left behind. Josie almost threw up as she saw human heads sliced open and their brains removed, to be eaten like prime caviar by creatures from another world.

A telepathic wave! Josie realized. The creature was so arrogant, so sure of his power, that he was telling us what we would do to us, she thought.

"Not on my watch," Josie screamed. But even as she whipped out her Glock, the creature read her mind and fired off a blast, Josie ducked and ran behind the bus as another blast rocked it.

"Oh, God," Josie yelled in dismay. The second blast had sheared off a back corner of the bus, leaving the supply compartment exposed. Suddenly she knew what to do. Just as the creature rounded the bus, an evil leer on its skull, Josie flung a canister of oxygen at it. Then she fell to the ground and covered her eyes.

Just as she expected, the creature fired at the canister. When his blast hit the oxygen under pressure in the canister, it set off a loud, fiery explosion of light and power. The creature hadn't been prepared, but Josie was. As it fell, she rushed it, snatching up its blaster before it knew what happened.

"Let's see how you like your own dish, jerk," she snarled as she fired the strange gun. Half the alien's body evaporated as the blast hit it.

Again and again, she blasted it.

She knew it was dead when the buzzing stopped.

Josie's sudden violence had left even her friends in awe. Now they could only stare as she grabbed a shirt from the ground, dipped it in the creature's blood, and used the blood to draw a maple leaf next to its steaming body.

* * *

After the battle, instead of unity division began to rear its head. And the leader of the dissenters was none other than the perpetual grouser, Bettie.

"The world has changed, and we have to change with it," Josie said as she cleaned her gun.

"We must find people, our kind of people," Bettie said. "Normal people."

"There is no normal, life is what we make it," Josie said. "We have to make new routines, making sure we are in possession of all our thoughts, trusting each other, having faith in ourselves and others."

"It's your fault, Josie, yours alone," Bettie said. "If we had stayed in Florida, we would have been rescued by the powers to be, you know, like the government or police."

Josie didn't answer Bettie as she continued berating her. She nodded at Bettie, not quite trusting herself to speak, then walked away with a group of people loyal to her following. Bettie's voice of discontentment hung in the air. A rabble of voices, hyper and flustered as strain and worry took hold, contused to debate the next step.

"Let's all talk it over with each other," Fred suggested. "After a night's sleep let's come together with suggestions and offers of experience, knowledge and understanding."

They posted guards with three-hour watches, then those who could went to sleep under the stars, at the site of Josie's victory over the alien.

Later that night, as others slept, Bettie continued to plot.

"I don't have to take it anymore," Bettie said to Lynn.

"But Bettie, listen to me, listen to me… Josie has done the best she could," Lynn, said. "Think of what happened to me. Without Josie I know I couldn't stay sane."

"See, what happened to you was Josie's fault, she wasn't there for you," Bettie said. "We can find a town, set up for protection. Life would be better. I know it would be."

"No, no she is watching out for all of us," Lynn replied.

"Then, why is she going north, only north?" Bettie said. "There could be and probably are civilized areas in all directions. Come with me. I know I can find people. I'm not stupid you know."

"I want to stay with Josie, she has a gun for me and others," Lynn said. "She's protecting us. You see how she saved us from that thing today."

"She pretends to look out for us, but it hasn't happened, has it?" Bettie said. "Well, why isn't she teaching you to shoot with her gun, huh, huh?"

"Remember when she gave us lessons at that carpet place?" Lynn said.

"Yeah, but nothing since then. I think she judged us and found us wanting—you notice how she sucks up to that Sandra and that new guy, Fred. You're not looking at the big picture," Bettie said. "Josie is only thinking of herself, finding the exact place to hide, ha ha. We should have stayed in Florida."

"Okay, okay, damn it, okay. I'll go with you." Lynn,

A group gathered around Bettie, listening. Several turned away for more sleep, but three young boys decided that Bettie was right.

In the early hours just before dawn, Bettie, hushing everyone, gathered them together.

"We have no food or weapons," complained Rich, a young teenager.

"I'll find food and shelter," Bettie said, "just stick with me."

In the breaking dawn, Josie uncovered the disappearance.

"Bettie has left with Lynn and three teenagers," Josie said.

"They left of their own free will," Fred said. Katie, who had been with Lynn, Josie and Bettie from the start, hung her head. She had grown to dislike Bettie, but she would miss Lynn.

"All we can do is wish them luck and hope they find what they are looking for."

Chapter 17

Three hours of walking later, Bettie's group tramped across a broken-glass-covered parking lot to an abandoned store. They had no problem breaking in, the door was dangling by one bent hinge. As they entered, the rotten smell of garbage and hordes of buzzing flies greeted them. But they were used to that by now.

"Gather up what looks good," Bettie shouted. "Everyone can look after themselves." After a few minutes, they tumbled out with armloads of chocolate bars, cans of pop and bags of chips.

As they trudged on, Lynn spoke up.

"Aren't we going in a circle? I'm sure we passed that burnt car before."

"No, no, we're headed where help is," Bettie snapped.

One of the young boys tripped and stumbled. He snatched at Bettie's arm for support as he fell.

"Get your stupid ass up, look after yourself," Bettie snarled. "Do I look like a babysitter?"

What a piece of snot, thought the boy, as he brushed himself off and moved on. Soon he slipped away, eager to return to Josie's protection.

Tony, a lanky teenager just turned thirteen, thought he heard funny noises. Not wanting to make extra noise, he gave Bettie's shirt a tug. Bettie whipped around, grabbed him by the upper arm, and gave him a violent shake.

"Don't you dare touch me," she yelled. "I'm not your babysitter."

Tony moved away, embarrassed and angry. Bettie didn't heed the changing mood around her.

"I'm stopping here to rest a while," she said. "It's so damn hot my feet hurt."

They followed Bettie inside an auto repair shop. The building was hot, with no plumbing or water. The boys hooted and hollered, ransacking the office for keys to the cars. Nobody was concerned about group safety, instead each found a place in a car in the shade. Soon most of them had dozed off.

Hours later, Lynn shook Bettie awake. She opened her eyes to find her group staring at her.

"What's for supper?" Lynn asked.

"What do you mean, what's for supper?" Bettie said with a yawn. "Find something, feed yourself, I've got my dinner." She pulled six Twinkies out of backpack, then went off to a corner to eat alone.

The boys had come to realize that the freedom Bettie offered was anarchy. They now knew they would have been better off staying with the larger group. They drifted away during the night.

The next morning Lynn woke early. After scrubbing herself as best as she could with some wipes, she pulled out her last chocolate bar. Then she nudged Bettie awake.

She waited for Bettie to make a suggestion regarding the coming day. Bettie wandered outside and headed up the road. The wind was blowing colorful clothes like confetti.

"Where are you going?"

"To find purple," Bettie said. "I want to be covered in purple, a sign of royalty."

Lynn knew it was time to rethink her options. She looked at the sky. The sun had risen, and she knew that it rose in the east. She faced the rising sun, knowing that left meant north.

She decided to leave Bettie, defy a nutcase, and head north towards Josie, towards hope, life, and sane, caring companionship.

* * *

Meanwhile, Josie and the rest of the travellers spent another sad evening, thinking of their missing friends.

"What more do we need?" Josie asked as they sat around a fire. "People to love and cherish, food, water, clothing, lots of that flying around."

The group members laughed, then quieted as Josie continued.

"Shelter and dreams of tomorrow," she said. "Yes, dreams, will we find home, our families?" And on that somber note they all headed for bed.

In the morning, they partnered up and made plans to scout the town off exit 288. One of the Plains survivors had once lived in the area, and he described the town ahead as a prosperous one—at least it was before the phenomenon.

Suddenly a phone rang. Few of them had heard that sound in a long time. Those who had cell phones were checking them. It was Katie's phone. She nervously put it to her ear, amazed that she still had both a battery and a signal.

"Hello? Hello?"

"It's me," Lynn sobbed.

"Lynn, Lynn, where are you guys?"

The mood picked up as the people gathered around to hear what they could of the conversation.

"I've been following our signs on I-75 for days, searching cars for food, water or a phone," Lynn said. I'm at a filling station with a pay phone that actually worked. I remembered Kate's number, thank God."

"We're near Carterville at exit 288," Katie said.

"I'm at Cobb's place, exit 269. Please, oh please, wait for me."

"Are you with Bettie and the boys?"

Lynn sobbed in huge breathless gasps. "No, I'm alone…so alone."

"Someone will meet you at the exit," Katie said. "We'll wait. Lynn, understand, we'll wait."

Everyone shouted and waved to get Josie's attention as several volunteered to go meet Lynn at exit 288.

Jeffery, a middle-aged man, stepped forward.

"I'm going, so back off everyone," he said. For once, Josie was glad to meet someone as bossy as she could be.

"She's about twenty miles away," he said. "I'll start heading her way and maybe meet her halfway, maybe further down the line."

"Here," said Sandra, giving him some extra water and a pile of protein bars.

The group was in good spirits as they talked of Lynn's return. No one mentioned Bettie. They quieted down after bidding Jeffrey good luck.

Then they turned toward Carterville. A group of them turned the other way up Main Street. Several townspeople met up with them. After the experience in Plains, Josie and the original travellers were cautious. But the hugs, handshakes, and welcome wishes were underscored by ear plugs, which the greeters handed out with a simple command:

"You need these."

"Why?" Josie asked. She got it right away, but wanted it verbalized for the group.

"Well, it's like this, that buzzing or low humming that's out there... it's a signal, a call or something. All we know is when it begins, we hide and plug our ears. If we don't, people go missing."

That jibed with what the travellers had seen. Josie remembered when it had all started, with the buzzing in Lynn's ears that made her go crazy in Port Charlotte.

The group spent the day scouting the town. They met other townspeople, a band of fifteen lonely people who still hoped for a better life. Many had lost family and good friends who had disappeared, one by one.

It was early in the day, with the sun just flooding the sky with soft pinks and faded orange edged by gray, a sign of a good hot day coming. The group fanned out to search abandoned houses and cars for food.

Josie and three others were in an empty house, when a man ran at her. Automatically she went on the offensive, striking out with her left arm, her right arm across her chest for protection. She crouched down as the body of a skinny male flipped over her.

"Josie, Josie, it's me," he yelled. "What's wrong with you? Roger sent me to get you."

She grabbed the man, who she recognized as one of the group that had joined them on the interstate. I'm sorry," she said. "We're all so punch-drunk lately."

"Josie, come quick," he said, brushing off her apology with a smile. "Hurry!" Then he took off running down the street.

"We're coming, we're coming," she yelled as Josie and her companions ran in pursuit. After several blocks, she turned a corner and stopped. She gawped in amazement and what lay before her.

There, at the train station, was a glorified monster of shiny steel and aluminum, red and blue, vibrating, telling them she was ready to go.

"Josie, a group out scouting had come across the train station," Roger said. "And guess what? There sat this Amtrak train pointed north. Fred said he would get it going. Look Josie, ain't she a beauty?" he added with a grin a mile wide.

"We can get everyone aboard," Roger said.

"Never in a million years would I have thought of a train for transportation," Josie said. "But with our group becoming larger and larger, why not?"

Things kept getting better. A shout announced Jeffrey, who, along with Lynn, walked towards the train station.

"I have never seen a more beautiful sight, dirty travel-weary Lynn," Josie thought as she thanked heaven her friend was safe and sound. There were hugs and kisses, roaring welcome from everyone. The group decided to make one more day of it in the town before heading out. That night, Josie lay awake, thinking of the future.

"We can't say here," she mumbled. A night of celebration, a sharing of the little bits of food found, had left her drowsy, but happy.

Lynn slept deeply beside Josie.

The next morning, it was all aboard. Fred, who appeared to be an expert with all engines, and Roger, a townsman who once worked the railroad, separated some coaches. Just the sound of the train moving had everyone excited. He left two coaches on, a working train.

"We'll see at the schedules how far she can take us," Josie said. She saw that the train was headed for Chattanooga.

"Pass it on," she shouted. "Bring any supplies, blankets, weapons, water, and food."

Marvin, a short, burly man who carried himself like a general, walked up to Josie.

"Ma'am, there's something over here I'd like to show you," he said.

He motioned for her to join him over at a large Army truck. In the back, he pointed out seven .50 caliber machines guns, boxes of ammunition belts, M-16s, grenades and other weaponry.

"Wow," Josie said.

"Yes ma'am, Marvin replied. "Wow is right. Look, a few of the boys and I are in the reserve— some of them saw action in the desert—I'm a Nam vet myself, so we know what to do with this ordnance. If you don't mind, I'd like to load this stuff we found over at the armory on the train—it might come in handy."

Josie thought of her single-handed fight against the alien. She knew luck and God had been there for her. But a machine gun would have helped.

"That's fine with me, general," she said.

Marvin blushed. "Aw shucks, I barely made sergeant."

"But you're our general," Josie said with a smile.

She grabbed some red paint and painted a huge maple leaf on the station wall. With the help of others and some ladders, she painted a second maple leaf eight feet high on the side of the train.

After a hurried round-up, everyone, men, women and children are on board. A voice boomed over the intercom, "All aboard."

The train slipped away from the platform. In calm relief Josie looked back at the bright red maple leaf on the station wall.

"Victory! Home!" someone shouted. In response there was an enormous commotion of voices, clapping, stomping.

"We're on our way," cried little Sammy.

As they moved towards Dalton, Georgia, Josie, ever vigilant, asked them to join her in practicing chants to guard against the buzz.

"Josie, let us rest," called out several voices.

Chapter 18

At the rear of the first coach, one tired older man with a four-inch gray beard started vomiting. People moved away. He looked up at Josie.

"Sorry, I feel sick."

She heard moaning and groaning with more nausea and vomiting in the next ten minutes.

"These people are really sick, plus some were vomiting due to the stink of vomit," Maggie said. "Could it be a flu or chemical poisoning or food poisoning?"

Sandra began attending to the sick people. Josie let Roger know.

"We're four or five miles from Dalton," he said. "We'll be stopping there real soon."

They glided into the train station in Dalton. They laid the sick people out on the platform.

They noticed pallets of bottled water, a blessing—there must be a bottling plant nearby. They found the address of the bottling plant on one of the pallets. A group set out to find the plant and bring back more water.

They returned with water as well as 20 folks who lived in an abandoned bread factory. They were reluctant to approach the larger group because of the strange illness but were quick to give them trays of fresh-baked bread.

Soon death was at their door. Two people died before morning. The next day, two more. By day six, they had lost twelve to this sickness. No death on day seven. They piled the dead in the park and cremated them with a few comforting words. Sandra diagnosed the disease as food poisoning. Apparently, many of the townspeople had made the mistake of eating contaminated food.

Soon it was time to move on. They had found food and water in the town, but they had also been followed by death. No one wanted to stay and the people in the Dalton were glad to see them leave.

It was time to move on. Roger, their conductor, supervised a group loading cases and cases of water, bags and bags of bread and muffins. He had two coaches and a boxcar loaded with weapons and ammunition. A huge red maple leaf decorated each side on the train.

Someone had painted the same sign on the train's platform. They were family.

The train rolled through the night. All were silent, consumed by the tragedy of the past few days.

Daybreak awakened some the next morning. As light seeped into the train, a heavy mist rolled over the fields. Those awake woke up others. Water and bread were passed around. No one was sick. They dined in whispered pleasure. Things were looking up.

Many miles after breakfast a smell of smoke surrounded them, a gagging stink that caused burning eyes. Everyone looked for an explanation, something. Volunteers handed out more water. Some people grabbed pieces of fabric, wet them, and covered their faces.

"Keep your cool, we're almost out of the city." Roger said over the intercom. Ten minutes later Roger announced, "We are entering the suburbs, almost out of that stinking hellhole. We have caught the spur to Nashville."

The intercom hummed again.

"Josie, a group of people are walking along the tracks behind us, about a mile or so."

Buzzing started in her head. I saw others listening to their minds.

"Blow the whistle long and hard," Josie shouted to Roger. In between the blasts she explained to everyone that the humming meant bad guys were trying to tune in and take control of minds.

"Do the alphabet song, rhyming, the sing-songs, anything," she shouted. Some folks pulled out the earplugs they had been given and stuffed them into their ears.

Oh, oh, we've fallen down the rabbit hole, Josie thought. We had won, yes, we had won the battle but now, the rest of the war.

"Josie, do you see the column of people, close to two hundred, walking parallel on the left?" Katie asked.

She swept her binoculars along the column. A sight to behold, several American flags and wow, a Canadian maple leaf. She stopped and blinked— was that Clint? She looked again, and the man was gone, lost in the large group approaching the train.

Wishful thinking, she thought.

Cars and dead people formed a blockade ahead on the tracks. Fred applied the brake, then yelled on the intercom, "Brace yourselves, brace, there is a blockage on the track. I'm slowing, hope to stop in time. Brace yourself now."

Everyone held on to someone. The buzzing continued. The buzzing had not stopped. The train slowed as brakes screeched and sparks flew.

Bump! The train gave a slight jerk as it kissed the wreck, left the track, and slowly jack-knifed. No one was hurt, but the train ride was over.

"Holy shit, Josie, look to the right," Roger shouted over the intercom. An army of ragged blank-faced zombies marched in perfect step about a half mile away, the earth shook with their steps. Behind them, as if herding the people, were several of the huge aliens like the one Josie had destroyed.

"Men and women, get the weapons from the boxcar," Roger yelled. "Get those Thompson submachine guns, load up with ammo, I'm coming to help."

Josie pulled the blaster she had taken from the alien out of her bag, where she had kept it hidden. Marvin set up his men and soon they were ready, boxes of ammo present at each machine gun site. The group following the train took up positions alongside it. Marvin's boys had a machine gun parked on the side of a coach warbling a steady song of death at the aliens.

The aliens approached, the travellers waited as they got near.

Most of them waited until the enemy was closer. Most of the pistols had a range of a hundred feet.

Josie saw that the humans being herded were dazed. They began to stagger away as the bullets from the train began reaching the aliens.

"Get down," Josie screamed at the people. "Down, down, crawl to us, keep low."

Another alien down. Cheers erupted as the feeling of power surged among the fighters. Hope was riding their shoulders. The gunfire intensified. Another alien down. The newly freed people took matters into their own hands and surged like a mighty mudslide over the last alien.

The fire fight died out, leaving deadly quiet under a rising cloud of acid-smelling smoke.

A voice rang out, "We're okay, they're dead. Damn dead." Sobbing and cries of joy filled the field as people advanced towards the train. Josie and the train's riders stream toward them, grabbing, hugging, and celebrating victory.

The battle was over.

* * *

As they walked toward the center of the battlefield the people gathered up their dead heroes.

Josie saw several American flags fluttering in the wind. She stood with tears in her eyes gazing at the trash pile of dead aliens with the staffs of Old Glory rammed through their bodies.

She silently thanked the many who stood true. Sandra set up a triage station on what was left of the train. Several doctors and nurses stepped up to the challenge of tending to the wounded. Other volunteers rounded up the confused humans left damaged from the mind control aliens. Many were comforted by many.

The dead were placed with love and respect along the right side of the train to be cremated as soon as possible.

Josie turned to make her way back to the train. She gazed back at the battlefield and gave a silent thanks to all. A light touch and a whisper startled her.

"Josie, Josie my love. I've found you."

"Clint, oh Clint." The lovers wrapped their arms around each other and squeezed with joy.

At dawn, they walked slowly past the burning funeral mounds. With respect and honor they paused to give final thanks to the brave fallen, knowing they would never be forgotten.

Chuck, a history buff, mentioned that their fight had been fought near Franklin, Tennessee, where a great battle had been fought during the Civil War. Josie asked Chuck to begin a journal of the great war they had just won.

The aliens were left burnt where they had fallen. The humans took no joy in their removal, no courtesy was shown the invaders.

"Where do we go from here?" Josie asked Clint as they settled in for the night. "Home seems very, very far away."

"You are my home, Josie," Clint said. "We'll make this our home, we'll search for a large academy or college that will house all of us. There must be several in this area. But as long as we are together, I will always be home."